A BOND OF HOPE

BOOK SIX

SACRED BOND GUARDIANS

LEE TOBIN MCCLAIN

GRACE PORTER BOOKS

1

Esperanza Acosta felt uneasy. She had felt that way all day, and now as Friday afternoon faded into evening, the feeling was growing.

She tried to ignore it as she checked on the twins, relieved to find them still sleeping after a restless day. In the past three months of caring for them, she'd learned that the moment one awakened the other would too.

"Hey, I'm home!" The voice of Esperanza's foster sister Rhonda echoed through the high-ceilinged rooms of their old Victorian house. Esperanza quickly closed the door to the twins' room, but a murmur from Ethan's crib told her she had five more minutes, at most, before they both were wide awake and ready for an active evening.

She smiled and shook her head. Rhonda would never learn to be quiet. And raising twins would never be a simple thing either, but she loved it. It was the closest she had come to fulfilling her most cherished dream.

Rhonda started clomping up the stairs in her gladiator-style high heels, and Esperanza leaned over the banister to hush her.

But a loud, happy cry from behind the twins' closed door told her it was no use.

"Uh-oh." Rhonda stopped mid-clomp, then shrugged apologetically at Esperanza. "Sorry. Did I wake them up?" Then, as Emmie's high-pitched giggle chimed in with Ethan's, she said, "Dumb question, I guess. Lemme get out of these shoes and I'll grab 'em, or one at least. Did you call off work?"

Esperanza followed Rhonda to her room and flopped down on Rhonda's bed, leaning back on her elbows. "I took a vacation day. My last one." As she said it, she searched her mind quickly: was that why she had been feeling uneasy? Because it would be harder to take care of the twins without the cushion of vacation time from her job at the adoption agency?

But she'd planned it all out, was considering taking her home business full time soon. Until then, she knew how she would arrange for their care when both she and Rhonda had to be at work. No, it wasn't that.

And it couldn't be Wayne. She and Rhonda had kept their move back to the suburb of Cleveland fairly quiet, and their phone number was unlisted. Besides, the last she'd heard of their evil stepsibling, he was living out of state.

Again she pushed the nervous feeling away.

Rhonda sprayed powerful-smelling perfume over every visible inch of flesh and traded her shoes for another, almost equally uncomfortable-looking pair. "Let's get the little buggers."

"Great. Thanks." Esperanza didn't even bother questioning Rhonda's clothing choices. Ever since the time when, as teenagers, they'd been thrust in a room together and told they were sisters, they had known themselves to be opposites, in fashion tastes as well as almost every other way.

And just like biological sisters, they'd learned to love each other anyway.

As they carried the babies downstairs, the sound of loud whistles and chirps from the back room told Esperanza her birds were ready for their dinner too. Raising parrots was her part-time business, but she loved them almost like they were kids.

Esperanza took one quick whiff of Ethan's sweet, powdery aroma. Then, after putting him into the musical swing set he loved—despite the duct tape that held its vinyl seat together—Esperanza hurried back to the bird room and picked up her favorite Amazon parrot, Buster. "You guys wait your turn," she said to the twenty-some birds whose cages lined one wall. "Babies first." She put Buster on her shoulder and headed back to the cluttered living room.

Rhonda sat with Emmie on her lap, spooning baby food into her mouth. Ethan was chortling in his swing, and the birds sang and chattered from the back of the house. The domestic scene made Esperanza's heart swell with contentment and love.

She had grown up without a real family, and had always longed for one. Raising babies was her fondest dream. As she went to pick up Ethan, she realized that she did have a family. An odd one, but a family.

Ten minutes later, the sound of the doorbell pierced her contentment and brought back the uneasiness that had plagued her all day.

～

GABRIEL MONTANA instantly recognized the small, dark-haired woman who undid the chain lock and inched open the door on the run-down Victorian house.

Esperanza Acosta. The receptionist at Open Arms Services where he had just taken over the directorship. She was attractive; his pulse quickened just looking at her, and that didn't happen to Gabe too often these days. But she definitely wasn't his type. She was intense, guarded, and she seemed perfectly happy to break the agency's rules.

When Esperanza recognized Gabe and the social worker he'd come with, her eyes narrowed. "Sadie. Mr. Montana. What's up?"

"It's your lucky day, Esperanza," Sadie sang out in a cheerful voice, tossing back her blond curls. "We're here for the twins. The adoptive parents are—" she glanced back toward the four-by-four parking at the curb—"right behind us."

Esperanza blanched, still keeping the door mostly closed. She looked back into the house behind her, seemed to draw a deep breath, and then turned back toward them. "Sadie," she said in a controlled voice. "You're supposed to notify the foster-care provider first, remember?"

"I did. I e-mailed you at the office yesterday."

Esperanza swallowed, her dark eyes enormous and shiny, and then spoke again. "I wasn't at work the past two days."

"Oh, my gosh, that's right!" Sadie clapped her hand to her forehead. "Esperanza, I'm so sorry. I've been out of the office so much, I forgot. We've been talking to that one family we'd worked with awhile back, the Roudabushes? Anyway, their circumstances have changed to where they're ready to move forward, and everything checked out . . . well, anyway, here we all are." She looked at Gabe apologetically. "Bad day to have the new boss along. My mind's like a sieve."

Esperanza took an audible breath. With obvious reluctance she pulled the door the rest of the way open. Gabe saw that she was dressed in cut-off shorts and a sweatshirt, and the sight of those slim, brown legs made his mouth go dry. To distract himself, he focused on the small parrot on her shoulder and the infant she held in one arm. And on the fact that she didn't look any too welcoming.

"Let me get this straight," Esperanza said through the screen door. "You want to take the twins tonight?"

"That's the plan," Sadie said. "The Roudabushes drove here from Columbus, and they're all set to go . . . Eppie, I'm sorry, but can we still take them? They don't have that much stuff, if I remember right."

Esperanza bit her lip and shook her head. "I don't see how it can work. A whole load of their clothes is in the washer now. I haven't bathed them yet. And you don't even want to see how the house looks."

Gabe hated to take away the authority of one of his workers, but this situation was too unprofessional. "Look, we'll get a hotel room for the Roudabushes tonight. We can come back and pick up the twins tomorrow, after Esperanza has had some time to prepare."

"Oh, but we were so hoping—" Mrs. Roudabush said from behind them.

"Agency policy requires twenty-four hour notification," Gabe said firmly. "Come on, let's leave them in peace for the night. *Lo siento,*" he added to Esperanza, but she didn't seem to recognize the Spanish apology.

Sadie and Mr. Roudabush turned, but Mrs. Roudabush walked up to the screen door and stood staring longingly at the baby in Esperanza's arms. Her husband turned back and took her arm. "Come on, honey," he said. "There will be all the time in the world, starting tomorrow."

The group started off down the steps. "Hey, wait a minute," Esperanza said, and they all turned back. She shifted the baby's weight and stood up straighter. "Since you're here, we may as well go ahead with it."

"Oh, Eppie, that would be great," Sadie said.

Esperanza straightened her back like she was trying very

hard to be practical and calm. "Those clothes in the washer. I could dry them and send them to you..."

"That's fine. We probably wouldn't use those clothes anyway," Mrs. Roudabush said. Then, looking at Esperanza's raised eyebrows, she hastily added, "Not that there's anything wrong with your baby clothes. It's just that we already have closets full of stuff for them. My friends at the hospital gave me a big baby shower yesterday, after we found out for sure about the twins."

"Mrs. R's a radiologist," Sadie explained to Gabe. "In fact, they're both doctors."

"Eppie, get in here!" called a woman's voice from the other room. "The baby just puked, and it's *purple!*"

Esperanza rolled her eyes. "You know she doesn't like plums," she called back into the house, and then turned toward the small crowd on her porch. "You all can come in."

Gabe looked at Esperanza. "You're sure about this?" he asked.

"Yeah, I'm sure," she said, nodding as if to convince herself. "What difference will a day make?" She held open the door, and they all moved into the narrow hallway. "Uh . . . go on in the front room while I put the bird away," she said. "You'll have to excuse the clutter. We haven't had much chance to clean up."

That was an understatement, Gabe thought as they crowded into a small living room littered with toys, crackers, and baby clothes. But at least, underneath the clutter, the floors were polished and clean and there was no dust.

And on an end table was a well-worn Bible bristling with sticky notes. Interesting.

The woman who'd called out before was there, her red hair impossibly frizzy, her leather skirt short, and her green fingernails so long that he feared for the infant she held. "Hey," she said without introducing herself as she scrubbed at a stain on her skirt.

The Roudabushes looked around at the disaster zone that passed for a living room and couldn't quite conceal their surprise. The father-to-be looked like he wanted to grab the baby away from the redhead. From the back of the house, a chorus of squawks pierced the awkward silence in the room.

"Um, I guess that bird she was holding wasn't the only one she has?" Mrs. Roudabush said, making polite conversation.

"Uh-uh. She raises 'em," the redhead said. "Rich people pay big bucks for the little critters."

There was another uncomfortable silence. Gabe wondered why Sadie, so highly recommended by the previous director, wasn't doing anything to smooth things over. He also wondered why the agency had placed the babies in this chaotic home, even temporarily.

Esperanza finally came into the living room minus the parrot, cradling the baby. Her eyes were red.

Something in the tender way she held the infant made Gabe ashamed about judging a messy house instead of the loving care inside it. It also made Gabe think of Melissa and the way she had held their child. He spoke quickly through the sudden tightening of his throat. "You haven't met each other before?" he asked, and when they shook their heads, he made a mental note to look at the agency policy. It would be better for all involved if the foster caregivers could meet the adoptive parents at least once before handing off the children.

"Gee, I'm sorry, I forgot to introduce you all," Sadie said, and did so, quickly.

"So you're both doctors?" Esperanza asked.

"Yes. But I worked out a way to take a leave of absence," Mrs. Roudabush explained. "I want to stay home with them, so John has agreed to be the family breadwinner for awhile."

Esperanza nodded. "That will be great for them."

"Can I hold her?" Mrs. Roudabush asked eagerly.

Esperanza looked down at the baby she held, and a muscle under her left eye twitched. Unaccountably Gabe felt like comforting her for her impending loss.

"She means this century, Eppie," said the redheaded woman, who had been introduced as Rhonda, some sort of relative of Esperanza's.

"Oh. Sure." And Esperanza held the baby out to the other woman. "Watch out," she said quickly as Mrs. Roudabush clutched the baby close to her chest. "She doesn't like to feel restrained. Here, just hold her loosely." She moved the other woman's arm into the proper position.

"Here, wanna hold one?" asked the redhead, offering her baby to Mr. Roudabush. "Good, this works out. I was gettin' ready to go out, and they've been so fussy, I hated to leave Esperanza alone with 'em." She shoved the child into Mr. Roudabush's arms, where it promptly started screaming. "I'm gonna miss the little buggers, though," she said over the din, tickling the baby's chin with a long green fingernail.

"He likes to be held against your shoulder," Esperanza said, turning to Mr. Roudabush and showing him how to shift the baby upright. "There, now jiggle him a little bit. Easy, like. That's it."

A car-horn honked repeatedly outside. "That's my ride," the redhead said. "I gotta go. Bye, everybody. Good luck with the kiddoes. I'll be in late," she added to Esperanza.

"Do you have a box or something?" Sadie asked Esperanza. "I can start packing their clothes. I know where their room is."

"I got them suitcases," Esperanza said. "They're in the bedroom closet."

"Oh, hon, you didn't have to—"

"Nobody should move from place to place with just a cardboard box."

"Well, they're not moving from place to place now," Mrs. Roudabush said as she looked lovingly at the tiny baby. "They're staying put."

"I'll go pack the suitcases," Sadie said.

Esperanza started picking up toys and infant clothes as soon as Sadie left. "You wouldn't believe it," she muttered to Gabe, "but this place was actually clean yesterday."

"Can I help you?" he asked to distract himself from how pretty she was. He stepped forward, and heard a crunch. "Oh, sorry."

"Ry-Crisps," Esperanza said. "Emmie loves to throw them at Ethan. Maybe you'd better just sit down."

He sank down onto the slipcovered couch and looked away from Esperanza. The Roudabushes stood cooing over the babies, inspecting them, talking quietly together. The scene was so loving and domestic that it made Gabe flinch inside. He'd taken this job because he knew the agency was in trouble and needed his business expertise. Plus, he had been ready for a change from high-powered consultant lifestyle that sounded so glamorous, paid so well, and involved spending most of one's time in soulless hotel rooms. He wanted to settle down, to actually live in the apartment and hometown that had become just a pit stop to him after Melissa's death, and to do something he believed in.

He believed in building families. But he hadn't bargained for the painful memories newly-formed families would stir up.

When he looked up he saw he wasn't the only one. Esperanza had grown still as she watched the Roudabushes admiring the babies. There was so much pain in her dark eyes that Gabe stood up quickly. He felt that he should offer some sort of comfort.

But he stopped himself. He wasn't her friend and wasn't

going to be. It would be best if they got this over with and left as soon as possible, for everyone's sake. "Is there anything you need to tell them about the babies' care, before they go?" he asked her, more abruptly than he'd intended.

"Do I have time to teach them the lullabies they each like best?" she asked without looking at him. "Or show them how to get Emmie to eat when she's fussy? Or tell them how Ethan likes nature, even as little as he is? How long would it take to pass on everything about two little personalities? Do you all have that kind of time?"

"I'm sorry you weren't told beforehand," he said. "This must be difficult for you."

She turned to face him. "Gee, all the girls at the agency were wondering about the new director," she said. "Now I'll be able to tell them that underneath the stone face, you're really a sensitive guy."

Ignoring the "stone-face" dig—he'd heard it often enough in the past couple of years—he met her eyes evenly. "I know pain when I see it."

She scanned him from head to toe, taking in his golf shirt, khakis, and docksiders. "You don't look like you've known a lot of pain," she said.

"Appearances can be deceptive."

She studied him silently for another moment, and then looked away. Her lips twisted as if she might cry, but she pressed them tightly together. He didn't expect her to say any more. When they got like that, women usually either had to clam up or burst into tears.

But Esperanza surprised him by offering a shaky smile. "I know, you're right about appearances," she said. She nodded toward the Roudabushes. "Take them. Rich doctors, but probably they're adopting because they can't have children of their own."

"This is a blessing for them," Gabe said, feeling another tightening in his own chest as he saw the couple exchange joyous, intimate smiles.

Esperanza nodded and took a deep breath. Then, like a prisoner facing her own execution, she walked over to the Roudabushes. Her back was straight, her shoulders squared. "You're welcome to call me anytime if they're doing something weird. I've had them for the past three months, and I've gotten used to their habits."

"Thank you," Mrs. Roudabush said, smiling, her eyes shining with tears. "Oh, honey, thank you for taking care of them for us." She reached out awkwardly to hug Esperanza, with the baby clutched in between them.

Esperanza returned the hug, but broke away quickly, and brushed her fingers beneath her eyes. She busied herself with finding paper and pencil, and then she and Mrs. Roudabush sat down to make notes about the babies' schedule and eating habits.

Courage. Sensitivity. It didn't jive with the previous image he'd had of Esperanza.

He remembered how, coming out of his office on his very first day at Open Arms, he had seen her whispering rapidly to one of the agency's clients. In fact, the two women had appeared to be arguing. A moment later, the client had promptly turned around and walked back out the door.

He'd introduced himself to Esperanza and asked her what was going on, a little peeved because he'd been planning to sit in on the counseling session with that particular client as a part of the orientation he'd set up for himself.

"Maybe our new decorating scheme scared her away," Esperanza had joked, gesturing at the half-stripped wallpaper and the pile of delivery boxes stacked by the door.

Given the intensity of the whispered argument he'd just

witnessed, Gabe knew it wasn't about decorating. But he was new on the job, and he wasn't about to make any accusations before he'd gotten the lay of the land. He held his tongue, but he'd decided to keep an eye on Esperanza. Especially since the former director, ousted in the midst of controversy and scandal, had left a note in her personnel file describing her as uncooperative.

It wasn't hard to keep an eye on Esperanza; she stood out from the long-term residents of Hopewell Corners, Ohio in both looks and attitude. Her dark coloring differed from the German-Irish look of most residents of the small suburb. She was tiny, barely over five feet tall and quite thin, whereas most of the folks around here had a well-fed look that came from plenty of meat-and-potatoes meals.

Unlike the other employees of the small collection of agencies, most of whom had known each other for years, Esperanza was quiet and guarded. She was polite, and seemed well-respected by the other staff members, but she didn't take her coffee break with them. Instead, she usually hurried out of the agency's front door and returned, out of breath, at the last possible second of her twenty-minute break. It had all made him a little suspicious.

Sadie came back into the room with two shiny suitcases, one pink and one blue. "They're all packed," she said. "And, Eppie, I put the formula and bottles in a box I found in the kitchen. Is there anything else we should take?"

Esperanza moved quickly around the room, grabbing a tiny sock, a stuffed rabbit, and a vinyl bathtub book in the shape of a boat.

"They're a little young for reading, aren't they?" asked Mr. Roudabush, smiling.

Esperanza shrugged. "You can't start too young. And they're smart babies, I can tell already."

"Oh, they'll be geniuses by the time we're finished with them," he said.

Mrs. Roudabush smiled at him. "I just want them to be healthy, happy children."

"Healthy, happy Rhodes Scholars," her husband corrected.

Esperanza had finished gathering the small items, and now she was tucking them into the suitcases. She closed one, and opened the other to slip a small blanket in.

"Don't worry about sorting the things out," Sadie said. "I'm sure it will all get readjusted once they get the babies home."

"Yes, and we've got a hundred more toys and baby things at home," Mrs. Roudabush said. "Enough to fill up both their bedrooms."

Esperanza went still in the middle of closing the suitcase, and Gabe frowned. Obviously toys and space were limited here, and the Roudabushes seemed unintentionally to be rubbing in how much more they had. Though Gabe had grown up with plenty of material wealth himself, he'd always been taught not to flaunt it.

After a moment Esperanza finished closing the suitcase, set it upright, and stood up. "If you have that many toys, think how messy *your* house is going to get," she said with a brief smile. "But seriously, Emmie really likes that one particular blanket. It helps her go to sleep. And they sleep better in the same crib, too, at least they have for me."

"Okay," Sadie said briskly, "are we ready?"

"Absolutely." The Roudabushes, each holding an infant, headed toward the door. Sadie picked up the little suitcases, and Gabe hoisted the box of formula, bottles, and diapers.

Esperanza sidled past them all to hold open the door. The Roudabushes hurried past her and started down the front walk. Then Mrs. Roudabush turned back. "Thanks again, honey," she called.

Esperanza just waved without saying anything.

Sadie put down the suitcases and squeezed Esperanza's shoulders. "Thank you so much," she said, "and I'm sorry I didn't get the message to you beforehand."

"It's okay," Esperanza said.

Gabe shifted the box to one hand and held out his right hand to her. "Thank you."

She hesitated and then shook his hand, and he marveled at two things: its tiny size, and the calluses that roughened it. He looked into those dark eyes, wondering how deep the contradictions ran in her.

She looked away and pulled her hand from his, immediately crossing both arms over her chest. "See you guys later," she said in a gruff voice. "Good luck with . . . with . . . the babies." And she turned and went back into the house, closing the door behind her.

Gabe realized suddenly that he had left his briefcase inside. Well, he would just have to get it when his hands were free. Actually, he wouldn't mind the opportunity to talk with Esperanza for a moment more—just to get a better take on her situation, for future reference.

But first he carried the box out to their new-looking four-by-four and watched Sadie help tuck the babies into their top-of-the-line car seats. And then they waved as the Roudabushes drove away.

"Whew," Sadie said, "that was a little awkward. I wish Esperanza had known we were coming. I don't always screw up like that, honest."

"Mistakes happen," Gabe said, "and after that experience, I'm sure you'll be extra careful in the future."

"Yeah. Well, look, my car's right down the block. I have to go fix dinner for my own little girl."

"I'll walk you down there."

Sadie smiled up at him and tossed back her hair, her voice going husky. "You're quite a gentleman."

Gabe realized his mistake too late. "I had it drummed into me from an early age," he said in a neutral voice as they started to walk, "that you shouldn't let a lady walk alone after dark. And this isn't the greatest neighborhood."

But Sadie still sounded provocative. "In fact, I have a couple of steaks in the freezer. If you want to join me for dinner . . . you being alone and all . . . I could feed Lydia real quick and get her to bed . . ."

"That's a nice offer," he said quietly as they reached her car, "but I have a few things to take care of at the office before I go home."

"Maybe another time?"

"You know," he said, "what I'd like to do is a cookout for the whole staff before the weather gets cold."

"Oh." She paused and seemed to digest what he'd said. Then she shrugged. "Okay, well, see you at work, then."

He watched as Sadie got into her car and drove off.

And then he was startled by a voice behind him. "That was a close one," Esperanza said.

He turned to face her. "I really do have a few things to do at the office."

"I'm sure," she said. "But that cookout idea was good. You must have some practice at making excuses to women."

Gabe shrugged, embarrassed. The truth was, since he'd lost Melissa, women did come on to him pretty often. Nice women. Pretty women. But he just couldn't work up any interest.

Esperanza's smile belied her reddened eyes, and she kept up a light, bantering tone. "I have to warn you," she said, "the girls at the agency are mighty intrigued about the new director. So quiet, so serious, Latino good looks. You're the latest topic of lunchroom gossip."

Gabe didn't know how to respond to that, nor to the slightly forced sound of her joking. He changed the subject. "You shouldn't be out walking alone either, you know. It's not the best neighborhood."

"I do it all the time. Here. You left your briefcase in my house." She held it out to him.

"Thanks," he said, taking it and wondering momentarily at his own disappointment. "I would have come back up to get it, eventually. But I thought you might need a few minutes to yourself."

For just a minute a window opened in those dark eyes, and Gabe was looking into that pain again. Then he thought he'd imagined it, because Esperanza smiled sardonically. "Well, well," she said. "Walking women to their cars, being sensitive to their feelings... *all* the girls will be chasing you."

"Except you?" Gabe didn't know what made him ask the question, and he regretted it immediately.

She backed away, hands lifted. "Not me, not hardly. But I do want to get on your good side."

"Why, because I'm your boss?"

"That's one reason."

"And the other?"

"Because I want you to give me a baby of my own."

The words shot straight into Gabe, creating an explosion of conflicting feelings. Esperanza, for her part, blushed red. "I didn't mean... I mean to move my adoption application along faster. Now that you're in charge, you have the final say about whether or not I get to adopt a baby. That's all."

"Of course." But the upshot of her comment was that he was more aware of Esperanza as a woman than he should be, considering that she was his employee.

2

The next morning, Esperanza backed her small hatchback up to the donation center, waved to the attendant, and started unloading.

Three bags. All that was left of Emmie and Ethan.

Last night had been rough. Esperanza was still reeling from the sudden loss of the precarious family she'd built. It didn't help that she kept remembering Gabriel Montana's eyes on her. For someone who seemed stiff and unemotional, he had seen through her cynical act too easily.

She pushed him out of her mind, just as she was trying to push out Emmie and Ethan. This morning, she had ruthlessly cleaned out their little bedroom. She'd folded the portable crib and stowed it in the attic, moved the dresser that had served as a changing table, and scrubbed down the floor and walls. The clothes she had left were tiny preemie things the twins had outgrown, too small for any baby she was likely to foster—or, God willing, adopt—in the future.

It was hard to put the bags down. But she reminded herself that it was better for someone else to get the use of them.

"Hey, Esperanza! Get over here and give me a hand!"

She dropped the bags and turned. When she saw the short-cropped, iron-gray hair and rosy cheeks of her friend Bessie, she felt her first smile all day. She hurried to help the older woman with the overflowing box of blankets and towels she was attempting to carry toward the donation bin.

They left the box with the attendant and then turned toward their cars. "Headed for work?" Esperanza asked, nodding at Bessie's white uniform and the nametag from the Valley View Senior Center.

"I've been working," Bessie said. "This is stuff from a new resident's home. She brought way too much when she moved into Valley View, and she's finally agreed to get rid of it. So I said I'd bring it over here before lunch. What about you? Where are those babies?"

Esperanza looked away, hoping Bessie wouldn't see the tears that suddenly burned her eyes. "They're gone," she said. "I was bringing ... some of their stuff over here."

"Oh." They had reached Bessie's car, and now they paused. "Did they go to a good family?"

"Couple of doctors," Esperanza said.

Bessie nodded briskly. "Okay. So you're a free woman. Why don't you come have lunch with me at Valley View?"

"Well ... I was going to finish cleaning today."

Bessie draped a strong, comforting arm around Esperanza's shoulder. "There's plenty of time for cleaning. You can take an hour off for lunch. We've got catching up to do. And besides, I have a project for you."

Fifteen minutes later they were seated at a window table in Valley View's spacious cafeteria. Esperanza couldn't help laughing as she looked at the tray in front of her. "I can't believe you made me get all this food," she said. "I'm not even hungry."

"You need your nourishment," Bessie said firmly. "You're too skinny. What man is going to want to hug a bag of bones?"

Esperanza laughed. Bessie was nothing if not blunt, and she had been known to hurt people's feelings with her sharp comments. But Esperanza had known Bessie for years—the woman was really her closest friend, despite their age difference—and she preferred Bessie's honest style to fake niceness any day of the week. "Thanks a lot. Luckily, I'm not looking for a man to hug me."

"I know, I know, you're fine on your own. All the more reason for you to keep your strength up."

"All right, I'll eat every bite," Esperanza said. "Or try to."

As they ate they chatted. Bessie, a practical nurse in Valley View's chronic care unit, had some difficult cases; but she always saw the humor in her work and found a way to make it enjoyable. Years ago, when Esperanza was a lonely foster child living next door to Bessie and her aging father, that positive attitude was one of the things that had drawn Esperanza to the older woman.

Bessie turned the conversation back to Esperanza. "How's Rhonda?" she asked. "She still living with you?"

Esperanza nodded. "Yes, and I don't know what I would have done without her during the last few months. She helped so much with the twins."

"Well," Bessie said, "she should help you. Knowing you, I doubt she's paying any rent."

"She can't, not yet. But she has a job interview this week."

"And you think that's gonna make the difference?"

Esperanza shrugged. "I don't know. Rhonda has a hard time looking past today. But she's got a good heart, and brains, and if she settles down, she'll be okay."

"And you're the person to help make that happen?"

"Why not? Lots of 20-year-old college girls run back home to Mom and Dad when they get into trouble, and nobody thinks anything of it. Rhonda's only problem is she can't afford college, and she doesn't have a mom and dad to run to."

"Except you're not her mom. You're only, what, twenty-five yourself. Don't let her take advantage of you because she was your foster sister for a few years. She might need a kick out of the nest sometime."

"We'll see," Esperanza said, digging into the large piece of cake Bessie had made her put on her tray. "Anyway, you never liked Rhonda."

"It might have something to do with all the times she borrowed money from my purse when you two were kids."

"Rhonda's over all that now," Esperanza said. "Hey, this cake is good."

"Yeah, well, keep track of your money," Bessie said. "And speaking of money, how's the bird business going? You making a profit yet?"

"More than I expected. And I'll make a lot more once this set of eggs hatches and I can sell the babies. But I'll be pretty busy hand-feeding the baby birds. I can't wait till I can do this business full time." She pushed her plate aside. "Hey, how's your dad adjusting to Valley View?"

Bessie shook her head. "It's tough giving up his own space. And he's mad at me for making him do it. But since that last fall he took, he's in a wheelchair. He couldn't manage that big three-story house."

"I didn't know about the wheel chair," Esperanza said, ashamed she hadn't stayed in closer touch with the man who had been like a grandfather to her during the two years she'd lived next door to him and Bessie. "Maybe I'll stop in and say hi to him. I have the time . . . now."

"You're going to miss those babies, aren't you?"

It was the first either of them had referred to the twins since the parking lot. Esperanza knew that Bessie didn't believe in dwelling on painful situations any more than she did herself. But the ache in her heart wouldn't go away. She nodded. "I know it was crazy, but I had some kind of hope that if I kept them long enough, my adoption approval would go through and—" She broke off, determined not to let her emotions get the better of her.

Bessie patted her hand. "I know you did, honey, but adoption applications take months, even years sometimes, and you just got started. You knew it wasn't likely."

Esperanza nodded. "I know," she whispered. "And I know they'd never give a single person two babies, anyway. But living with them day-to-day, I got to thinking of them as mine."

The older woman took both of Esperanza's hands. "I understand. And I know it hurts." She looked hard at Esperanza. "You been going to church?"

"It was hard with the twins, but we got there most Sundays." Between foster parenting and working and taking care of the house, it seemed like church was the only place she could sit still and see the bigger picture.

"Good," she said. "You keep it up. Now, what are you doing to get that adoption application moving?"

Esperanza frowned. "I finished the paperwork, and now it seems to be out of my hands. There's a new director—in fact, he came along last night to help pick up the twins—so maybe he'll move things along." Gabe had seemed like the type to take charge, though she had also seen how skeptically he had looked at her home and her things. She wasn't sure if his presence would be a plus or a minus for her adoption dreams.

"Right, Gabe Montana. I heard." Bessie started piling dishes onto her tray. "Well, I'd better get back to work. But if you'll come with me for a couple of minutes, I have a project for you."

"Uh-oh."

"I think you might like it. At least, I hope so."

After putting their trays full of dirty dishes on the moving belt into the kitchen, Esperanza followed Bessie to a back storeroom. As soon as they opened the door, they were rewarded with an ear-splitting shriek.

"A parrot?"

"Uh-huh."

Esperanza walked across the windowless room toward the sound. "Hey, honey, what are you?" she cooed to the ugly mass of feathers and bare-plucked skin. "It's a scarlet macaw. Where'd you get it?"

"A new resident," Bessie said. "She had been ailing for awhile at home, and her bird wasn't getting any attention. Just stuck in a back room for days at a time, except when somebody remembered to feed it."

"But macaws are intelligent!" Esperanza studied the bird inside its too-small cage. "They need a lot of stimulation. If they don't get it, they can start plucking their own feathers, like this guy did." Cautiously she raised her hand toward the cage. The parrot lunged at it, beak open.

"See? Nobody can get near it. And it screams and cries all the time. It's driving the staff crazy."

"And you want me to take it."

Bessie grinned. "Yep. You're the only person I know who knows birds, and maybe you can do something with it. The owner isn't going to be able to care for it, and none of her relatives can stand it, but she wants it to go to a good home."

"What's its name?" she asked, raising her hand toward the cage again. Again the bird lunged. As it stood in a threatening posture, beak open, her heart went out to the miserable creature.

"Paco. And you'd be doing us a real favor if you got him off our hands."

"Well . . . rehab cases are hard. I've never done it with such a big bird. But okay, I'll give it a try."

"I knew you would," Bessie said with satisfaction. "When can you pick him up?"

"I'll come back later this afternoon, after I clear out some space for him."

As they walked out Bessie said, "You ought to talk to that new director. See if he can move your adoption papers along. Gabe's a pretty nice guy, even if he does need to loosen up a little." She smiled. "Tall and dark and handsome, too."

Esperanza thought of Gabe's clean-cut good looks, his wiry, athletic build. Supposedly he'd been the best lineman the high school team had ever had, legendary for skill and strength even when Esperanza attended the same school ten years later. He still had the muscular body of a high-school athlete.

"So you know him? What's he like?" And then, lest Bessie think she was interested for herself, she added quickly, "Do you think he'll support my adoption case?"

"I know he's a good man. Maybe a little serious, but he always had to take care of his sisters and brother. His father died young, as I recall, and I can't imagine that unpleasant mother of his was much help. Anyway, I think he'll be fair."

"Maybe I should ask him to check on my application, then."

"Do it," Bessie urged. "You have to go for what you want. It's not gonna just come to you."

∽

But two days later, Esperanza wasn't sure that going to see Gabe was such a good idea.

The trouble started when Charlene McCall, an agency client, came in smelling like a brewery. Esperanza was at the reception desk, completing some paperwork, and she smelled the young woman before she looked up and saw her.

"I'm here for my meetin' with the job counselor," Charlene drawled.

"Not like that, you're not," Esperanza said in a low voice. "Go home, sober up, and come back tomorrow."

"Whaddya mean, sober up?" Charlene whispered. "I ain't drunk."

"Maybe not, but you smell like it." Esperanza came out from behind the desk to keep the conversation quieter. "The job counselor's never going to hook you up with a good job if he thinks you drink during the day."

"I smell—oh, Lordy," Charlene said. "This is the same shirt I wore to the bar last night, and somebody spilled beer on it."

"If that's all it is," said Esperanza, "you can run down to the dime store and buy a clean shirt. I'll lend you a few bucks. But if you had anything to drink today . . ."

Charlene looked down. "I did have a beer with lunch. Okay, two. Jimmy was drinkin' and I had to keep him company."

Esperanza shook her head. "I think you should reschedule for tomorrow," she said. "And don't have anything, I mean *anything*, to drink."

"Will you tell the guy I don't feel too good?" Charlene asked, looking ashamed. "It's the truth."

"Sure."

The moment the other woman had left, Gabe appeared at Esperanza's side. "That's the second time I've seen you send a client away," he said, his tone accusatory. "What's going on?"

"I didn't send her away, exactly. I just talked to her."

"And then she left. What did you say?"

Esperanza hesitated. She didn't want to get in trouble at work; she needed the job, and she needed Gabe to consider her a responsible person. At the same time, she didn't want to cause

Charlene any more problems than she already had. Esperanza knew that Charlene had a couple of kids and hadn't finished high school, and needed the services of the job counselor badly.

"She wasn't feeling well. I could see that, and I suggested that she come back tomorrow when she could make a better impression."

Gabe crossed his arms over his chest. "Shouldn't you let the job counselor be the judge of that?"

Esperanza had wondered the same thing herself. She was just the receptionist. But then again, she thought she had a little more sympathy with the things some of the clients were going through than the naïve, clean-cut, fresh-out-of-college job counselor. "Maybe I was out of line," she said slowly. "If I was, I'm sorry."

Just then Charlene came rushing back in. "Did I forget my bag in here?" she asked before she saw Gabe.

"Uh..." Esperanza tried to shield the woman from coming over by Gabe. "I don't think—" But it was too late. Charlene walked over to the chair by which she had, in fact, left a small shopping bag, in the process passing close to Gabe.

He stepped forward and introduced himself. "Are you sure you don't want to keep your appointment?" he asked Charlene.

"No. I'm sick," she said quickly, backing away. Then, clutching her bag, she hurried out the agency's door.

When she was gone, Gabe turned and looked hard at Esperanza. "Did you send her home because she was drunk?"

Esperanza met his eyes. Anything she told him about Charlene couldn't hurt the woman's reputation further. "Actually, I don't think she *is* drunk."

"Don't lie to me," Gabe interrupted in a harsh voice. "No one could miss that smell."

"Don't you dare accuse me of lying."

"What would you call it, then?"

"I'm trying to explain, if you'll give me a chance instead of interrupting and jumping to conclusions."

Their voices had risen, and Gabe looked around as if realizing for the first time that people in the back offices might hear them. "Let's take this discussion to my office."

Esperanza hadn't been in the director's office since the previous guy had left, and she was startled by the change. Instead of a massive dark wood desk dominating the room, Gabe had a normal-sized desk, a computer table off to one side, and a small conference table surrounded by four comfortable chairs. There were photographs, but instead of portraying him with important politicians, they all portrayed him with children: a middle school football team, a group around a Christmas tree, and an outdoor shot with a multi-ethnic crew of dirty, happy-looking campers.

It made sense that he would like children, given that he was now heading up an adoption agency, and it softened her heart a little. It helped, too, that after motioning her into one of the armchairs Gabe sat down, not behind his desk as she'd expected, but in a chair facing hers across the small table.

And then he spoke, and his judgmental tone wiped out the points his office décor had made in her mind. "Okay," he said, arms crossed over his chest. "You wanted to explain, so explain."

Esperanza reminded herself that she needed this man on her side. She took a deep breath and spoke calmly. "I know Charlene a little bit. She lives in my neighborhood. I've never known her to get drunk during the day."

Gabe's lips twisted. "A ringing endorsement of her character," he said. "I'm assuming that means she does get drunk at night?"

"What she does at night isn't really our business, is it?"

For a moment he just looked at her, staring her down. It was as if he didn't expect a lowly receptionist to argue with him.

"No," he said finally. "It's not our business what she does at night. But during the day, if she's using the job service—"

"I'm getting to that," Esperanza said. "Charlene said she was wearing the same shirt she wore out last night, and somebody spilled beer on it."

"And she didn't change her clothes?"

"Not everybody has a big closet full of clothes to choose from," she said, looking pointedly at Gabe's obviously-expensive shirt and tie.

"But when she's meeting with a job counselor..."

"Not everybody is used to thinking about making a good impression, either. For some people, at some times in their lives, just getting out the door in one piece is an accomplishment. And anyway, isn't that the whole point of our job service? To help people think through things like making an impression?"

"Yes, it is," Gabe said. "But our counselor never had a chance, because you sent Charlene home."

Esperanza hesitated, and then nodded. "I know. Like I said, maybe I was out of line. But—" She paused.

"What?"

"I just wonder if the job counselor might have jumped to the same conclusion you did," she said slowly. "I mean, not knowing Charlene's situation, and he's, you know, kind of young and all—"

"Younger than you?" Gabe asked, cracking the first smile in the conversation.

Esperanza shrugged. "I'm twenty-five. Anyway, there's young and young."

Gabe looked a little surprised. "True. Is there something about Charlene's situation that we should know?"

The intense, attentive way he looked at her made her feel flustered. "Well," she said, "Charlene's been having a rough time. With her kids, and her ex-husband, and money being tight. She's under a lot of stress."

"Go on."

"In all honesty, she told me she did have a beer at lunch, with her boyfriend. He tends bar, and I've heard he does drink kind of a lot. But she wasn't slurring her words, and she didn't look drunk."

"And you would know."

"What's that supposed to mean? Do you think I hang around with drunk people all the time?"

"Just the opposite," he said quietly. "You look too young to have much experience at all."

The sudden gentleness of his tone took her by surprise, and something in his eyes made her look away.

"Esperanza," he said. "I think I made a mistake calling you out for what you did with Charlene."

His eyes were as warm as his tone of voice, and she was so floored at the notion of a powerful man admitting he'd made a mistake that she just stared at him.

"What you were doing is technically peer counseling," he said. "You took a look at her situation, and gave her good advice."

"There's a "but" in there somewhere."

He smiled briefly. "Yes, there is. I would still like to see the clients get to their appointments. If there's a problem with a job counselor not understanding the clients or the situation, we need to attack that problem. Not cover it up by shielding him from all but the easy clients."

"But in the meantime, while he's learning, Charlene doesn't get off welfare," Esperanza argued.

"You have a point. I need to give some thought to supervision for those learning periods." He stood up. "I've been taking the staff to lunch, one or two at a time, to get to know everyone," he said. "I'd like to take you tomorrow, if you're free. It's also by way of apologizing for misjudging you before."

"That's a switch, the director taking a receptionist to lunch," Esperanza said. "Unless . . . " She looked at him quickly. "Just a professional lunch, right? That's all you want?"

Gabe reddened slightly, and his glance shot to a small photo on his desk, one she hadn't noticed before. "Just a professional lunch, believe me," he said.

Curious, Esperanza looked at the photo too. A beautiful blond woman, and an infant wrapped in a blue blanket. Strange —everyone said he was single. But she wasn't about to ask him about it. She, more than most of the people in this small-town office, understood the need for privacy about some parts of a person's life.

"Sorry to question you," she said, "but the guy you replaced was kind of a sleaze. Lunch will be fine. Maybe we can talk about my adoption application, if you get a chance to look at it."

He was watching her with curiosity and a little smile. "Some of the folks who work here get intimidated by the idea of a new director coming in from outside. But you don't, do you?"

"Should I be intimidated?" she asked, looking at him. His brown eyes had a rare depth and warmth.

"No, you shouldn't," he said, his usual impassive expression returning to his face. "I'm just an ordinary, fallible guy. More fallible than most, if it comes to that."

"And you even admit it. Okay, I'll see you tomorrow." And until then, she'd try to avoid obsessing about what might happen on their lunch date.

3

The next morning, when Gabe walked into the country-themed café where his sister worked, he knew he was running late; his friend Nick was already halfway through his usual steak and eggs. Usually Gabe arrived well before six, but this morning he'd drifted uneasily between sleep and wakefulness, disturbed by images of the woman he was taking to lunch today.

Romantic images, the likes of which hadn't invaded his dreams for three years.

And that was ridiculous, because it was just a business lunch, he reminded himself as he leaned against the counter, waiting for his sister to come out of the kitchen. He was Esperanza's boss, and he wouldn't even consider dating an employee. Besides that, he didn't want to start a relationship. Even if he did, it wouldn't be with someone like Esperanza. He liked simplicity and stability. And he had to admit to himself that he liked being in charge, and he liked a woman who needed him. Esperanza seemed anything but simple and stable, and she acted more self-sufficient than most women he'd known.

"Hey, big bro," Bianca said, coming out from the kitchen

with an oversized spatula in one hand. She was a pretty, delicate brunette, the baby of the family, and her pampered upbringing had prepared her more for a fancy office or being waited on in a mansion. But she insisted that she wanted to be a cook, and took it seriously enough that she was working part-time while she finished culinary school. She looked happy, too, as she spun around the counter and hugged him exuberantly.

"You're in a good mood today," he said, smiling.

"'Cause I met a new guy," she said, loud enough for Nick to hear back at the corner table. Nick just shifted his newspaper, ignoring her. Gabe grinned. Bianca and Nick had dated off and on since high school, prompted partly by the fact that Gabe dated Melissa, Nick's younger sister, and Melissa was Bianca's best friend. But while Melissa and Gabe had been class sweethearts, then dated through college, and then married right after graduation, Nick and Bianca had had a much stormier relationship. Now it was supposedly over, but from the way they still snipped and snapped at one another, Gabe had his doubts.

"Do I know him?" Gabe asked his sister. "Am I going to approve?"

Bianca shrugged. "If I were looking for your approval, I'd probably get it. He's the fire chief over in Laughlinville," she said.

From the corner, Gabe heard a distinct snort.

"He's a great guy, and he really likes me," Bianca enthused loudly.

"Bring him to Mom's for Sunday dinner," Gabe said, "so we can decide if he passes muster."

"Maybe I will," Bianca said. "Or maybe I'll wait until *you* bring somebody."

"You may wait awhile, then. I'll take my usual, when you get a chance." He turned and walked back toward Nick's table.

"Go ahead, change the subject," Bianca called after him. "But one of these days, you'll get bitten by the love bug again, if I have anything to do with it."

"That's the only bright thing she's said all day," grumbled Nick as Gabe sank into the booth across from him. "Dating the fire chief from Laughlinville. She must be getting desperate."

"Why don't you solve her problems and take her out yourself?" Gabe asked.

"No way. And don't change the subject. When are *you* gonna start dating again, anyway?"

"Not interested," Gabe said flatly. "Did you see McMichael's touchdown pass last night?"

"You're gonna get too old if you wait much longer," Nick said, ignoring Gabe's question. "What are you now, thirty-five? Going on fifty?"

Luckily, Bianca brought out Gabe's cereal and toast then, and Nick got distracted. Gabe grabbed a section of the paper and scanned it while the two of them bantered. They meant well. But even though they had both loved Melissa, they had decided that it was time for Gabe to be over her death and to start dating again, and they could be persistent about it. One or the other of them was always bringing some eligible woman to a family dinner or a party, hoping to pique Gabe's interest.

He just politely declined. They, of all people, should understand his reluctance to get involved again. He had failed miserably at protecting his family before. And since Melissa's death it was as if a heavy weight had descended on him, never to be lifted. He knew he was too serious, too rigid, but he couldn't go back to the open, confident man he'd been. The few dates he'd been on had fallen flat.

Fortunately, Nick and Bianca had enough issues of their own to keep them occupied. They barely noticed when Gabe finished his breakfast and headed out to work.

He was conscious of Esperanza all morning. He saw her efficiency in answering the phone and handling the numerous clients when things got busy. He noticed that she willingly helped those clients with children, and remembered that, according to Sadie, it had been Esperanza's idea to set up a little play area for kids in the waiting room.

But while she was good with the clients and great with kids, she kept her distance from the other secretaries and counselors who staffed the agency. She still didn't take her coffee break with the others, and she didn't join in their friendly gossip.

Just before lunch time, Gabe located the short version of Esperanza's adoption file and started looking through it. She had said she wanted to discuss it at lunch, and he decided he should be at least a little familiar with her case. The long file was with the administrator who would actually handle it and make most of the decisions. Only if there were a disagreement among the caseworkers and the administrator would the final decision come his way.

Everything was orderly. A plan was in place to do the home study. Her references had been interviewed; a local woman who raved about Esperanza's abilities with children, and Bessie Ingram, a woman Gabe knew from church.

That was all well and good, but he saw that Esperanza had no family in the area. She was single, and she wasn't well off.

He sighed. Esperanza was too much like the single girls and women who gave up their babies for adoption. From all the research he'd done before taking this job, he knew that not a one of them would choose her. They always wanted a two-parent, well-to-do family to give their babies what they couldn't. He couldn't understand why Sadie, or the previous director, hadn't explained that.

He was just starting to reread Bessie's statement when Esperanza knocked on the jamb of his open office door.

"Are we still on for lunch? I have to let Carrie know when I'm going," she said. She was wearing trim, dark slacks and an emerald-green shirt made of some silky stuff. Her dark hair, clipped back at one side, rippled down her back. Obviously she wasn't trying to look sexy, like some of the secretaries who seemed to be having a contest about who could wear the shortest skirt, but somehow she looked more intriguing.

Gabe snapped himself out of that thought, wondering where it had come from. "Let's go now, if it works for you." He stood up briskly, setting the adoption folder aside. If he wanted to know more, he could just ask her. It would give them something to talk about at lunch.

Thinking about lunch brought Bianca to mind. "Do you mind if we stop at my apartment for a minute? I need to pick up some tax forms for my sister."

"Um, that's fine, I guess."

"It's right up there." He gestured toward the brick building on the corner of the residential block ahead, then pulled into the parking lot, glided into his usual parking place, and stopped the car.

"You're welcome to come in."

"That's okay."

"You're sure?"

"I'm not going in your apartment. Got it?" Her tone was fierce.

Suddenly Gabe realized what she was thinking. "Are you worried that . . . Esperanza, I just need to grab some tax forms for my sister to sign. I help her with the accounting side of her business. I hope I haven't done anything to make you think I have an ulterior motive."

Crossing her arms over her chest, Esperanza fixed him with a dark-eyed glare. "You're the boss, okay? You ask the receptionist to lunch. Then you happen to drive by your apartment and find an excuse to stop. Here's where I'm supposed to act cool and relaxed, and come on inside. But you know what? I've learned to call them as I see them, and this to me is a questionable situation. So I'll wait here."

"Esperanza—" He broke off. Why was she so uptight about men, and him in particular? What did she think he was going to do, throw her down on the living room floor and have his way with her? "Fine. Forget I stopped." He started up the car again.

"Gabriel?" called a shaky voice from across the parking lot.

He sighed and rolled his window the rest of the way down. This day was getting more annoying by the minute. "Yes, Mr. Simpson, it's me."

The older man hurried toward Gabe's truck, hauling two bags of groceries with him. "You're home in the middle of the day. What's going on?"

"I . . . was going to pick up some paperwork for Bianca."

"Then why are you leaving again?"

"We changed our minds." Gabe glanced over at Esperanza and saw a grin tug at the corner of her mouth.

"Who's that with you, son?" Mr. Simpson peered past Gabe. "I don't think I know you," he said to Esperanza.

"Mr. Simpson, this is Esperanza Acosta. She works with me at the agency."

"Uh-huh," the older man said, nodding. "That was certainly convenient, that she planned to come up to your place." He looked Esperanza up and down. "You know, you're welcome to wait in my apartment. Unless there was some *particular reason* you wanted to spend the lunch hour in Gabriel's place?"

Oh, great, Gabe thought. It was obvious that his nosey neighbor thought Esperanza was another one of the gold-digging women who'd chased after him since Melissa died. Mr. Simpson meant well, and Gabe had known him for years, but the last thing Gabe needed was for Esperanza to get more offended than she already was. This lunch had been a really, really bad idea.

To his total surprise, Esperanza laughed out loud. "I'm glad to meet you too, Mr. Simpson," she said, leaning close to Gabe, which raised his blood pressure alarmingly. "Actually, I wasn't sure about going into a relative stranger's apartment. But with you to police us, suddenly I feel completely safe." She leaned back, opened her car door and got out.

Gabe shook his head and turned off the car again. He'd never understand women.

By the time he got out of the truck, Esperanza had come around to his side and was shaking Mr. Simpson's hand. "Haven't I seen you before?" she asked. "Maybe at church?"

The older man peered at her through his thick glasses. "Now that you mention it, I believe so." He put his grocery bags down and rubbed his chin. "I believe so. In fact, now I remember when you joined. Some Mexican name? Estella? You're not one of those illegal immigrants, are you?"

"My name's Esperanza." She smiled at the older man. "It means 'hope' in Spanish. And I probably know less about Mexico than you do. I haven't been lucky enough to learn Spanish yet, and I was born and raised in Cleveland."

"Uh-*huh*." Mr. Simpson looked Esperanza up and down again and picked up his grocery bags. "Gabriel," he said without turning toward him, "why don't you take the lady inside? You don't want to make her stand around while you gather up the paperwork you forgot." He turned abruptly and walked toward the apartment next to Gabe's.

Esperanza's dark eyes were full of laughter. "Come on, you heard the man."

Gabe rolled his eyes as he led Esperanza into his apartment. "Sorry about Mr. Simpson," he said over his shoulder. "He doesn't mean any harm, but he does tend to get a little overinvolved in his neighbors' lives."

She laughed. "I'd hate to be the woman who tried to take advantage of you on his watch."

"Be right back. Make yourself at home."

When he came back downstairs a few minutes later, she wasn't in the kitchen. Hearing a sound in the living room, he headed there and paused at the doorway. Esperanza stood, her back to him, studying something on his mantel. Her hair shimmered down her back in loose, shiny waves.

Rubbing his hands briskly together, he walked toward her. "Ready to go?" he asked.

Esperanza turned to him, and he saw that she had a framed photograph in her hand. "Your wife and child?" she asked.

Gabe nodded and cleared his throat. "They're gone," he said, hoping she wouldn't ask how.

"How long ago?"

"Three years."

She studied the picture for another moment. "She was beautiful," she said. "Looks just like a picture of an angel that was in one of the houses I lived in growing up."

"That's what I used to call her," Gabe blurted out. Then he crossed his arms over his chest and took a step back. He had never told anyone that before.

"What, angel?"

He nodded, embarrassed at having revealed such an intimate detail of his life with Melissa.

"You still miss her." It was a statement, not a question.

"Every day."

Esperanza nodded. Then she looked around. "Doesn't it make it worse, having all these pictures around? It's kind of like a... memorial, or something."

"It's not like a memorial," Gabe snapped. "I like it."

She shrugged. "That's fine. I just . . . whenever I lost someone, growing up, I guess I took the opposite approach. Got rid of the pictures, the reminders, the letters. I tried to block it out." She turned the picture over in her hands. "Like with the twins. That night you all came and took them away, I stayed up late cleaning out their room. And the next day, I donated most of their stuff to the Goodwill Center."

"You did?"

She nodded. "It hurt to look at it."

"For me . . . I think it would hurt putting it away."

Esperanza grinned. "Let me guess. When you take off a Band-Aid, you do it real slow. And when you get in the swimming pool, you do it one toe at a time."

"Right about the Band-Aid, wrong about the pool," Gabe said, smiling back at her. "I jump right in."

They stood there another moment, looking at each other. Gabe's words, *I jump right in*, seemed to hang shimmering in the suddenly-charged air.

"I'm different," Esperanza said slowly, "about the pool. It takes me a long time to get up the courage to go in." Her eyes never left his.

Involuntarily, Gabe stepped toward her, then stopped a safe distance away. He took Melissa's picture from her hand and placed it back on the shelf. "Let's go to lunch," he said to the top of her suddenly-bent head.

～

Minutes later they walked into the café where Bianca worked. "I might be a little biased," he said, "but I think it's the best eating in town." And it was bright and crowded and not at all romantic. It wouldn't promote these odd feelings he kept getting about Esperanza.

Gabe had brought several of his employees to lunch here already. But the quick, appraising look his sister gave Esperanza was different.

"I haven't met you, and I've met almost everyone in town," Bianca said to her after Gabe had introduced the two women. "Are you new around here?"

"Actually," Esperanza said, "we *have* met before. I was a year behind you in school for a couple of years, when I lived here in Hopewell Corners. We were in choir together."

"Really?" Bianca asked, sinking down into the booth beside Gabe. "What years?"

"Ninth and tenth grade, for me."

"It's strange I don't remember you. Not that my brain was especially sharp back then, but still..."

"I was pretty quiet," Esperanza said.

"And then your family moved?"

"Um, not exactly." Esperanza pushed at her water glass and then used her napkin to wipe up the ring of condensation it had left on the table. "I lived in a foster home. With the Grants, on Elm Street? When they split up, the kids got moved to different homes. Me and one foster sister ended up in Cleveland."

"That must have been rough," Bianca said.

Esperanza shrugged. "I was used to moving. But I always did like it here. When I was deciding where to settle down last year —after I got enough money together to buy a house—I knew this was where I wanted to be."

Gabe felt a little annoyed that Bianca had found out more about Esperanza in five minutes than he had in the weeks he'd known her. "Bianca, we need to order so we can get back to the office at a decent time," he said.

"Hey, loosen up," Bianca said. "You're the boss, aren't you?"

Gabe could tell from the way Esperanza grinned down at her coffee cup that she liked Bianca. "Yes, I'm the boss," he said to his sister, "which means I should set a good example, instead of staying out for two-hour lunches and keeping the employees out as well."

"All right, all right," Bianca said, getting up. She took the menus from them. "Have the meat loaf. It's really good today."

Gabe shrugged. "Okay with you?" he asked Esperanza.

"Sure."

"And I think you should bring her to Sunday dinner sometime, since it turns out we're old friends," Bianca tossed over her shoulder as she headed back toward the kitchen.

Esperanza looked startled.

"Bianca considers everyone a friend, or a potential friend," Gabe explained. "In her mind, now, you two grew up together." He didn't add that Bianca was also probably trying to fix them up.

Until their meals arrived, they made small talk about the town and the agency. Gabe almost hoped that the subject of Esperanza's adopting babies wouldn't come up. It would be hard to tell her that she wasn't likely to succeed in her quest.

But halfway through the meal, Esperanza put down her fork and looked at him. "Have you had time to evaluate my adoption file?" she asked bluntly.

"I took a quick glance at it," he hedged.

"And?"

Gabe saw the eagerness in her eyes and pushed his plate away half-finished. "How much has Sadie told you about what our birth mothers want?"

Esperanza shrugged. "A little," she said. "Mostly I worked with the old director. He told me I fit the profile perfectly, which is weird because the other agencies I looked at were really discouraging. But he said Open Arms is different, because it's not just an adoption agency. They're more used to looking at the whole person. And Sadie told me it was only a matter of time."

A Bond of Hope 41

Gabe shook his head slowly. He'd known the former director was unethical, but this was downright cruel.

"What? What's wrong?"

Gabe looked into her concerned brown eyes, looked away, and then looked back at her. "This is the problem. Most of our birth mothers are young, single women. And since there are so many more people who want to adopt, than there are birth mothers, the birth mothers get to choose the adoptive parents."

"Right. I know that." Esperanza's eyes were glued on his face.

His hand even moved a couple of inches toward hers, but he forced himself to bring it back. "Esperanza," he said gently, "they almost never choose a single woman."

She stared at him a moment longer and then looked away. Finally she looked back at him. "What do you mean, almost never?"

"My understanding is that it's only happened once since the agency opened four years ago," he said.

"Only ... once."

He nodded. "And that was a situation where the birth mother knew the adoptive mother already."

Esperanza's hands tightened on the edge of the table. She stared down for such a long time that Gabe began to worry, hating to see her so upset even though he'd expected no less. He was about to speak when her heard her whisper something.

"What?" he asked, leaning closer.

She lifted her head to look at him, and to his surprise her eyes were dry. They were also furious. "That jerk," she repeated.

For a moment Gabe was puzzled. "Who?"

"The guy you replaced. What a complete, total jerk."

"Do you have any idea why he told you you fit the profile? And why Sadie didn't set you straight?"

Esperanza nodded slowly, her lip curling. "Oh, I have an idea, all right. I can't believe I was so stupid. I mean, I quit my other job and moved right down the street from the agency, getting ready." She dropped her forehead into her hand, elbow propped on the table. "Stupid, stupid, stupid."

"I still don't understand."

"Oh, he had a . . . *thing* for me. I guess he thought, if he told me what I wanted to hear, I'd be grateful enough to do all the sleazy stuff he wanted."

Despicable. Add it to the list of violations that had ousted the man. And suddenly he remembered the negative note the previous director had put into Esperanza's file. Either he had been angry about her being "uncooperative," as he'd put it, with his advances; or he was trying to protect himself against revelations like this.

Esperanza was ripping her napkin to shreds, her movements short and violent. "I should have known," she said.

"How could you know?" Gabe didn't like the self-criticism in her voice.

Her lip twisted again. "He was a jerk, like so many guys. I *know* that, but I let myself forget. And Sadie, well, she was kind of under his spell. She did whatever he said."

Gabe spread his hands, wishing he could take this incredibly mismanaged situation and set it instantly right. "Esperanza, I'm sorry. I'll report it to the board right away. And I'll look into the systems, make sure it won't happen again."

She flung the shredded napkin aside. "So what are you saying? That there's no chance at all?" Her eyes had gone darker, and he saw the pain there. Just like the night they'd taken away the twins.

He spoke quickly, wanting to wipe away that pain. "I'm saying it's so unlikely that you should be pursuing other options. Have you thought about public adoption? Older children?"

"Public adoption wouldn't work for me," she said abruptly. "Anyway, it's almost all older kids. And I want a baby."

"Can I ask why?"

Her dark eyes flashed lightening at him. "Nobody asks married couples why they want a baby, so why does everyone keep asking me?" she asked.

"Because you'll have a hard time getting a baby," he said, "whereas there are a lot of older children waiting for adoption. I would ask a married couple the same thing, because I feel for the waiting children."

"Yes, well, I feel for them too," Esperanza said, "since I was one myself. But I . . . have my reasons for wanting a baby."

Noting the sudden guardedness of her face, Gabe wondered what that reason was. He also knew it was likely to come out in the home study and interview process, so he didn't push it. "You're young," Gabe said. "Maybe later on, if you marry—"

"I don't want to get married!" Esperanza's voice wasn't loud, but its intensity drew the attention of the next table.

This time, he did put his hand over hers, wanting to calm her. "I'm sorry to be the one telling you all this," he said. "If your application goes through and everything checks out, we'll put it in the book for the birth mothers to look at. Maybe it will happen for you."

She looked at him for a long moment and then pulled her hand away. "But you don't think it will happen," she said.

"I don't think it will happen."

After a moment, she broke her gaze away from his and looked down. "I think we should go."

Looking at her bowed head, the shiny black hair hiding her face, Gabe's heart ached. Not only that, but he was furious that this had happened, that a vulnerable woman had been lied to and hurt. He'd fix it. It was his job to fix it.

Which didn't help her now. "I'm sorry, Esperanza," he said. "I just thought I should tell it like it is."

She nodded without speaking.

"I . . . I'm sure you'll find a way to make use of your talents."

She looked up then, and her eyes burned. "I'll find a way to adopt my baby. You'll see."

4

A few days later, Esperanza emerged from the bird room at seven o'clock in the morning, yawning. She was surprised to see Rhonda already up and dressed and, apparently, jazzed up on coffee.

"What are you going to do when all those eggs start hatching?" Rhonda asked. Then she snapped her fingers. "Hey, guess what? Guess who called?"

"Who?" Esperanza went to the sink to wash her hands.

"Remember Maria, our little project in Waster Wayne's family?"

"Of course!" How could she forget the adorable seven year old they'd protected from Wayne? "She called?"

"Yep. She's all grown up and did her homework, and found us."

'How?" Esperanza frowned. She didn't want to be findable by anyone, because she didn't want to be findable by Wayne.

Rhonda shrugged. "Her husband's a police officer, I guess. Anyway, she's doing great and wants to come visit from Pittsburgh. Wants to thank us for everything, natch."

"That's so awesome!" Esperanza gave Rhonda a fist bump as

she headed for the coffee pot. They'd coached little Maria in how to act at an adoption picnic, scraped together money to buy her a beautiful sundress, and scanned the gathering for the best potential adopters. They'd decided on a slightly older couple, John and Annie Moretti, who lived in Pittsburgh, ran a school for boys, and seemed kind and loving and perfect for Maria. And then they'd proceeded to rave about what a good girl Maria was, kind and helpful and no trouble at all. Maria had done the rest with her dark eyes and high cheekbones and cute, skinny vulnerability.

It had worked, the Morettis had adopted her, but of course, they'd lost touch with their short-term sister. Story of a foster kid's life.

Remembering what they'd done for Maria, how they'd protected her from Wayne's increasing interest, and now having the chance to reconnect... all of it made Esperanza smile so widely her cheeks hurt. "It would be so, so great to see her again. I hope she means it."

Rhonda nodded. "I gave her our address, and she's going to text you to set something up." Typical of her distracted, jittery style, she switched subjects. "Anyway, how are you going to do your job and be home for the bird babies, too?"

"Just keep running down here on coffee breaks, I guess, until next month when I go part time. That's why I bought a house close to my job." Esperanza rubbed her eyes and reached for a mug. "Thanks for making coffee."

"I needed it, but now I'm too buzzed." Rhonda wiped the counter restlessly. "I can't believe you get up this early every day."

For the first time, Esperanza noticed that Rhonda wore a skirt and blouse, both somewhat conservative for her. "What are you doing up, anyway?"

"I told you, I have a job interview. You're such a space cadet these days."

"I'm sorry. Rhonda, that's great! Are you excited? Where is it?"

"Some warehouse over in Bay City. It's a part-time inventory clerk job, but it might go full time."

"Good for you. I know you'll get it."

Rhonda shrugged. "Maybe yes, maybe no," she said. "Anyway, what's happening with you and the adoption business? Did you talk to that guy Montana?"

Nodding, Esperanza said slowly, "We had lunch yesterday. It's not good news."

Rhonda ripped open a Pop-Tart and started eating it from the package. "Why, what's up? Aren't you supposed to be at the top of the list?"

"More like the bottom."

"What?" Rhonda's hand froze halfway to her mouth. "What happened?"

As Esperanza told Rhonda the harsh realities Gabe had confronted her with yesterday, Rhonda looked more and more disgusted. "So that old director was just trying to jump your bones?" she asked when Esperanza had finished. "Is that what it was all about?"

"That's how it looks." Esperanza wrapped her hands around her coffee mug. "I just feel so stupid. I can't believe I bought into his lies."

"Hey, we all get screwed over by men at one time or another. Welcome to the club." Rhonda leaned back against the kitchen counter. "So what's the deal with the new guy? Is there any way he could help you?"

"I don't think so. I mean, he feels bad, but what can he do?"

"Well," Rhonda said, "he's the boss. And I thought, from the way he was looking at you that night they came for the twins, that *he* might have the hots for you."

"No. No way. Anyway, what would that have to do with my adoption application?"

"Everything! If he thought approving it would get him closer to you..."

"I don't think he's like that. He's very..." Esperanza reached for words to describe Gabe, and came up short. "He's honest and, well, ethical."

Rhonda studied her for a moment, licking her fingers. "He took you out to lunch, right?"

"Yes. Just like he took all the employees out to lunch."

"Are you going to see him again, outside of work?"

Esperanza turned to the coffee pot to pour herself another cup of coffee. "Actually, I might go to his family's Sunday dinner next week, but he may not even know about it. It's only because his sister asked me—"

Rhonda was grinning openly now. "He put his sister up to it. He likes you. I knew it!"

"Oh, he does not."

"I bet you ten dollars he does." Rhonda scrolled through her phone, found a song, and turned it up. Then she tugged at Esperanza's hand, making up words: "Come on, Eppie, let's dance! Come on, Eppie, let's dance!"

"Stop it." Esperanza rolled her eyes and pulled away.

Rhonda stood looking at her, shaking her head. "You are so weird. Don't you get lonely? There are times when that little bed upstairs seems so cold, and I'm just dying for somebody to put his arms around me. Don't you ever feel that way?"

It was a serious question. And Esperanza felt like she had to try to make an impact on Rhonda, because they were the closest thing to sisters that either one of them had. "Sure, I feel lonely sometimes," she said. "But I don't think going out with somebody I'm not committed to is the answer. I think I'd just feel more lonely if I knew I was physically close with somebody I didn't love, or who didn't love me."

Rhonda sagged back against the counter. "Yeah. It does hurt when you need a guy and he's not there anymore. Most guys, just a whiff of trouble or a hint you're starting to depend on them, and they're outta there." She straightened up. "But that's men. Can't live with 'em, can't live without 'em."

"I can live without men," Esperanza said firmly.

Rhonda shook her head. "You're getting involved with this Gabe, whether you like it or not. He likes you, and I think you like him too. Geez, what time is it?" She glanced up at the kitchen clock. "I gotta get my bus. Unless you'll loan me your car?"

"Take it. I don't need it today."

After Rhonda left, Esperanza withdrew to the bird room for one last check before work. Once there, the birds' beauty and cheerful whistles soothed her, and their unconditional affection warmed her heart.

"Why can't people be more like birds, Buster?" she crooned to her favorite Amazon parrot, scratching its neck.

She thought about what Rhonda had said. She was *not* getting involved with Gabe. The fact that his sister had decided to befriend her had nothing to do with him. The trouble was that she was thrown together with him at work all the time. And he was so good looking, and seemed to be a kind, strong man; and the loss and pain he'd suffered made her sympathetic toward him.

Maybe that longing Rhonda had described was starting to catch up with her, because it did feel good to imagine Gabe's arms around her. And now, especially since the loss of the twins, she did feel lonely at night.

Esperanza started rearranging her shelves, frowning. She

had to face the fact that her emotions were tugging her a little bit toward Gabe. And that wasn't good.

She knew herself well enough to realize there wasn't much chance any kind of relationship would actually work. Court-ordered counseling had helped her to deal with some of the difficulties of her life as a foster child, but she knew very well how many scars remained. Whenever a man got close, she felt herself stiffen and retreat. The best solution she'd found was to keep her distance.

She needed to take some steps backward from Gabe. Now, before they got close.

She looked at Paco, the big red macaw. Between her job and the other birds, she hadn't spent enough hours with him. If she had the time, she knew she could rehabilitate him. She was *good* at working with birds, even gifted. With people, on the other hand, she lacked even the basic ability to form good relationships.

Checking the big calendar on the wall, Esperanza realized that two people were coming over the next day to look at birds, one at a baby Amazon that was almost weaned, and one at a cockatiel. That meant she should try to get home in time to clean the room thoroughly, not just the quick once-over she did every day. Customers liked pristine. But birds shed feathers every day.

Picking up the baby amazon, she petted it aimlessly and let it preen her hair, thinking. She had always meant to have this business turn full time. She hadn't expected it to happen for another year or so, but it was frustrating not being able to do the things she needed to do to grow the business. If she quit working eight hours per day, she could advertise, network at bird shows, get more birds . . . in short, she could make money doing what she loved to do.

But could she make enough money?

And wouldn't it be great to quit her job and stop worrying about Gabe?

Slowly she walked over to the desk where she kept her paperwork and accounts. She had meant to keep working until she could afford a great laptop and modernize all her bookkeeping, but if she stayed on paper for the next year or two . . . she checked her balances and thought of all the eggs that were about to hatch. If most of those birds lived, and she sold them all . . .

After another half-hour of studying her financial picture, she'd made her decision. She would quit her job.

The next evening, Gabe looked at the stack of files and paper in his "In" basket and sighed. It would be another late night.

But then again, that beat going home to an empty apartment any day of the week. He walked out to the candy machine to get fortification for a couple more hours of work.

On the way, he glanced out into the reception area. Most of the staff had already left, but Esperanza was still there. So she had the evening shift tonight.

As he picked up his candy bar from the machine's tray, he heard an exclamation from the lobby, and for a minute he thought Esperanza was calling to him. But as he walked out there he saw that Esperanza was squatting down by the play area.

"Tanisha, what are you doing there? Your foster mom left two hours ago! She's probably hunting all over for you."

"No, she ain't." The flat voice belonged to a stocky light brown girl of about eight years old. "She thought I left with Germaine. Besides, she doesn't care what happens to me."

"What have you been doing?" Esperanza scolded, but in a

softer tone. "I didn't hear you at all." She was still squatting down, and she looked all mother, firm but loving. Gabe wished moments like this could show up in an adoption application.

"I took me a nap," the child said. "Right there in that little playhouse."

"Well, you were quiet as a mouse." Esperanza patted the girl's shoulder. "I'm gong to call your mom and then take you home as soon as I clean up my desk. Don't you live pretty close by? I think I've seen you in the neighborhood."

Tanisha nodded. "But I want to go home with *you*."

Gabe thought it was time to get involved. Tanisha's foster care situation sounded problematic, but unfortunately, that wasn't within his jurisdiction. All he could do was try to find her adoptive parents as soon as possible, and he resolved to redouble his efforts. "Hello, ladies," he said as he walked into the reception area. "Anything I can do to help?"

Tanisha immediately backed away and looked down at the floor. "No sir," she mumbled.

Esperanza put a protective arm around the child. "I'm going to take Tanisha home in a few minutes," she said, "after I've finished up some filing. In fact, Tanisha is going to help me, aren't you?"

"What do you mean, help you? I'm just a kid."

"You know your alphabet, right?"

"Yeah."

"Then you can file."

Gabe watched, amused, as Esperanza showed Tanisha how the filing system worked. Within a few minutes she had the girl carefully putting folders into their proper places.

She made a quick phone call to Tanisha's foster mother and then came over and stood by Gabe. "Looks like we've got ourselves a new helper," she said.

He treasured the smile she gave him, the smile of two grown-ups over a child. He didn't know what impulse made him spoil the moment by saying, "But aren't those files confidential? No one but an agency employee should have access to them."

Esperanza rolled her eyes. "Gabe, she's not reading them, she's filing them. Lighten up." Then a thought struck her. "But, oh, Lord, what if she sees her foster mother's file?" She hurried over to the file cabinet. "Let me see those files a minute, honey," she said. Gabe watched as she extricated one file, then handed the stack back to Tanisha.

"What's that, Miss Acosta?"

"Just something I need to show Mr. Gabe. You're doing a good job, honey."

Tanisha smiled and resumed her task, and Esperanza walked back over to the doorway and stood beside him. "Thanks, Gabe," she said. "That was a close call."

"Still think I should lighten up?" he couldn't help teasing.

She tossed back her hair. "Yeah. I do. You're too serious."

He was looking at her, and an urge to pull her close came on him like the hunger of a starving man. Startled, he clasped his hands tight behind his back.

"What?" she asked.

"Nothing." He tore his gaze away from hers, afraid it revealed his heart. He'd better watch it, or he'd be just as much of a jerk as the former director. He would quit his job himself before he'd put her through that again.

"All finished, Miss Acosta!" came Tanisha's clear, high voice.

"Later, Gabe," said Esperanza, backing away from him. Gabe wondered if she'd seen something of his struggle.

Wanting to normalize things between them before she left, he said in what he hoped was an easy, comfortable tone of voice, "You're taking her home, then?"

"Yes. She lives just a few blocks from me, and it's a nice night. I think we'll walk."

"Is the neighborhood safe?"

"Lighten up, Gabe," she said, and with relief he noted that the smile was back in her voice. So his wayward thoughts were still his secret. "I walk a lot. We'll be fine."

After they'd gotten their coats and left, Gabe slowly wandered back to his paper-strewn desk. Now that Esperanza was gone, his desire to work late had abated too.

He was so drawn to her, it wasn't even funny. And it wasn't just physical, either. She wasn't intimidated by his position or his serious style like some of the other workers. When she bantered with him, or when he saw her with a child, he felt an incredible longing to wrap his arms around her.

Obviously, he needed a companion. Esperanza was around a lot, since they worked together, and she was attractive. Oh, not to everyone. He was sure there were plenty of men who liked a flashier, more openly sexy woman.

But for him, Esperanza's conservative, comfortable clothes were appealing. They said she didn't spend a lot of time thinking about her appearance or trying to draw the attention of every man in the room. She was comfortable with herself without needing wolf whistles or flirtation.

Her appeal wasn't something he should focus on. Not only was Esperanza his employee, making her entirely off-limits to him, but she was the opposite of the type of woman he wanted as a wife. She was the opposite of Melissa, delicate, dependent Melissa, who had needed his care. Esperanza didn't need anyone.

Or so she thought. Really, there was a deep vulnerability in her eyes in her few unguarded moments. But that was another thing. She was vulnerable because she had such a troubled past. Just look at that rundown place she lived in, that crazy friend, the childhood of moving from foster home to foster home. If a man broke through her defenses, what he would find was a heap of trouble.

No, a woman like Esperanza was not in his play book.

He shook his head, cleared a space on the desk in front of him, and started attacking his overflowing in-basket.

Fifteen minutes later he got to a letter that made him blanch.

Effective in two weeks, I am resigning my position as receptionist at Open Arms Services... Sincerely, Esperanza Acosta.

The words in the middle of the letter were a blur.

She was resigning? Why?

He scanned the letter again, but the vague, polite sentences offered no reason he could understand. She claimed to be pursuing other interests. What did that mean?

There was a knot in Gabe's stomach as he thought about working at the agency without her. He suddenly realized how much he depended on the chance to see her face, to hear her laughter as the clients' kids played around her desk, to experience her irreverent comments on his way of doing things.

But the knot in his stomach was about more than missing her. He was worried that she was quitting because of what had happened with the previous director, leaving in anger because she couldn't pursue her adoption dreams here. Even worse, he half-feared that she had seen his attraction to her and quit because of it.

If the agency's unethical former director—or he himself—was the cause of her resigning a job she needed, then he had to set that right.

Two minutes later he was on the street, walking in the direction of Esperanza's house. If she wasn't there, she was walking back from Tanisha's house, which according to the mother's file, was a few blocks along the same street.

Esperanza's house was dark, so he walked past it. On the

next block, three teenage boys looked him over, and as he approached, one made a quiet-but-rude comment in Spanish.

Gabe recognized the insult from the time he'd spent doing business in Peru. *"Que dice?"* he asked, keeping his tone neutral.

The kid, who he now saw was only about half his size, waved his hands and took a step backward. *"Nada, nada,"* he said quickly, and Gabe nodded and continued on his way.

He knows Spanish! The other two boys hooted at the one who'd insulted Gabe. But Gabe just frowned as their voices faded behind him, thinking about Esperanza walking here, alone.

When he saw her coming toward him in the half-light of a street lamp, he slowed down to observe her. She moved quickly, watchful of the people scattered on the streets and porches.

No matter what she said, she *was* afraid, walking in this neighborhood after dark by herself. As well she should be. Gabe suddenly wondered how many of her other tough stances concealed fear.

As she approached, he said her name. She stiffened and looked up, a canister of pepper spray in hand.

When she recognized him she stopped, a relieved smile crossing her face. "It's you," she said.

"Ready to defend yourself, I see," he commented, indicating the pepper spray. He turned and walked beside her. "Why'd you act like it was no problem walking here alone?"

She shrugged. "I do have to walk here sometimes," she said. "Especially now, since Rhonda's looking for a job and borrowing my car. So... I got myself some protection. No big deal."

"You're scared," he said quietly.

Frowning, she started walking again, and he fell into step beside her. "What if I am? Some things scare you, but you do them anyway."

They reached the trio of boys who'd spoken to Gabe before.

He noticed how Esperanza stiffened and sped up, and he moved fractionally closer to her and kept pace, nodding at the boys as they passed them.

One of them called something after him. Sounded like a question about whether Esperanza was his lover.

"*Si, esta de mio,*" he called back loud enough to be sure they all heard him.

"What did you say to them?" Esperanza asked once they were out of earshot.

Gabe hesitated. "They wanted to know if you were my girlfriend," he said slowly.

"And you told them I was?" she asked, sounding incredulous.

"Yes. I did. Only because it might be a good idea if the men around here think you have somebody to protect you."

"I don't need protecting."

He changed the subject. "Don't you understand Spanish?"

She shook her head. "I was going to take it in high school. Then I was switched to a vocational school that didn't have languages, and that was that."

"But—"

"I know, my name and coloring. I'm Latina by birth, obviously, but I never had any Spanish-speaking foster families. So I never had the chance to learn Spanish. Did you learn it at home?"

"A little, before my father died. He was Cuban and Spanish was his first language. He wanted us kids to be bilingual, but he passed on too soon."

"Your mom?"

"She never learned it. But I was interested, so I studied it in high school and college. And then when I worked in business, I traveled to South America pretty often. I had a chance to practice with native speakers quite a bit."

"Yeah, well, I bet the businesspeople you worked with didn't talk like those jerks," she said. "They're a nuisance."

Gabe tried to keep his mouth shut, and then couldn't. "Why do you live here, anyway?" he asked. "This neighborhood isn't a very good place for a woman, or even a couple of women, to live alone."

She glanced up at him. "Okay, college boy, I'll give you three guesses to figure out why I live there."

"It's cheap."

"Hey, you got it in one guess! You must have gotten all "A's."

"And there's probably another reason, or there was. It was close to your place of employment."

They had reached her house now, and Esperanza stopped to look up at him. "You got my letter," she said.

Gabe nodded. "I did, and it came as a surprise. I want to talk to you about it."

Esperanza glanced up toward her house, then back at him. "Can it wait until tomorrow? I need to feed my birds."

Gabe felt awkward pushing her, but he also thought her backing away from him might have to do with her reasons for quitting. And he thought of her claiming to be brave about walking the streets alone, and carrying her pepper spray.

"If you really have to get something done, I can wait," he said. "But I'd rather talk it through tonight, if not now, then later. Because I'm wondering if your quitting has anything to do with the agency's mishandling of your adoption application." He hesitated. "Or with me."

5

Esperanza froze in the process of fumbling through her handbag for her keys. Gabe's question rang in her ears. "No, of course not," she said quickly, a reply that sounded defensive even to her. "I just . . . well, it's a long story, why I need to quit."

"I'd like to hear it," Gabe said quietly. "I feel responsible for the agency and how it treats its employees and clients, and I know there was real injustice in your case."

"That's not your fault. It was before you ever worked there."

"Doesn't matter. I'm still responsible." There was stubbornness in his voice. If she didn't want him hounding her for the rest of her time at the agency, she was going to have to explain. Gabe obviously wasn't going to give up.

She might as well confront it now. "Okay. Do you want to come in?"

"Are you comfortable with that?"

She knew immediately why he'd asked: because she'd been so reluctant to go into his apartment with him. But now, she realized, she *was* comfortable with him. At least in the sense of not thinking he'd do something dishonorable.

"Sure, I trust you," she said. "Come on in."

Gabe followed her into the house. "Where's your roommate?" he asked.

Esperanza shrugged. "Out, I guess. Rhonda doesn't spend a lot of time sitting at home."

"Do you go out with her much?"

"Not really," she said, hanging her coat on a hook in the closet. "I'm not much of a drinker, so it's not as much fun for me. What everyone else at the bar thinks is funny, I just think is stupid. I turn into a real wet blanket, so I usually just stay home." She took his coat and hung it up.

"Sounds familiar," Gabe said. "Did you mean it about feeding your birds? Because I can wait."

"Actually, if you don't mind . . . " Esperanza could hear the birds calling from the bird room at the back of the house. "They always hear me come home and they want feeding and attention." She hesitated, unsure of whether to treat Gabe like a friend or a boss. But their conversations, about both her adoption plans and his past losses, had brought them closer, and after all, she was getting to know his family. "Do you want to come with me while I feed them?"

"Sure, I'd like to see them. My mom kept parakeets when we were growing up. I like birds."

Esperanza led the way to the back of the house. Before opening the door she turned to him. "Now don't . . . they're birds, okay? They're a little loud. And messy."

"I think I can handle it," Gabe said.

So she ushered him inside and made quick rounds, greeting each bird or pair as she refreshed their feed, scratching Buster's neck, checking on the nesting pairs and eggs. "Oh, Sunny, they're about ready to hatch, aren't they?" she cooed to a lutino cockatiel who'd clambered off the nest to check out the fresh feed. "That's it, stretch out. You've been sitting there all day, haven't you?"

The cockatiel bent its head so Esperanza could scratch it. "Yeah, you need some lovin', don't you?" she whispered. Then, conscious of Gabe watching, she continued moving from cage to cage.

When she got to Paco she stopped. "Hey, guy, how you doin'?" she asked.

The big red bird eyed her cautiously.

"Wanna come out?" She opened up the cage door, then turned to Gabe. "We go through this every day. He's been neglected, and I'm trying to rehabilitate him. He won't come out, but every day I give him the chance."

"Are you sure about that?"

Esperanza looked back at the cage and gasped. Paco stood on the edge of the doorway, which was further than he'd ever come. Slowly she raised her arm to him and, after a slight hesitation, he stepped on.

"Good boy, Paco. Oh, what a smart bird!" She praised him extravagantly to reinforce the behavior. "Gabe, could you hand me a peanut from that green shelf?"

But as Gabe walked slowly toward them, Paco bent his head and gave Esperanza a vicious bite on the arm, just below the end of her short sleeve.

"Ow!" she couldn't help crying out, but she immediately stifled the reaction. Any dramatics might make biting seem exciting to Paco, and if he got into that habit he'd be impossible. She reached for the cage door.

"Do you need help?" Gabe had approached them, and Paco bent toward him, hissing threateningly.

"Gabe, go back over by the door, okay?"

"Are you sure? Can you handle him?"

"I'm fine, just move away."

Gabe did as she said, and she carefully put Paco back into his cage, blinking against tears of pain. The bird sat on his perch and nonchalantly began preening himself. Only after she'd closed the cage door did Esperanza look at her badly-bleeding arm.

"That little stinker," she muttered as she grabbed a handful of paper towels. "Come on, let's get out of here."

Gabe followed her into the kitchen. "That looked painful. What happened? Why do you keep such a vicious bird?"

Esperanza ran water onto fresh paper towels and held them to her upper arm, wincing. "Believe it or not," she said, "that was real progress in there. Paco hasn't come out for me before."

"Yeah, and then he took a bite out of you. I wouldn't call that progress."

"I think he was jealous of you."

"So he bit *you*?"

Esperanza nodded. "That happens a lot with parrots. They're pretty complex. They displace their jealousy or anger onto their favorite person, a lot of the time. And the thing is, up to now Paco hasn't had a favorite person. Since he bit me, I think he's maybe starting to bond with me."

"Love hurts, eh?"

"Yeah." Esperanza looked up at him. Gabe was standing right next to her and both of them were leaning against the kitchen sink. All of a sudden she felt that *heat* again—the thing she'd felt in his apartment and a couple of other times they'd been close to each other. Her heart beat harder.

"Let me look," he said in a curiously tender voice. He pulled the towels away and studied the area, displaying no distaste for the ugly wound with traces of blood still seeping from it. He refolded the paper towels and pressed them gently against her arm again. "Do you have some antibiotic cream?" he asked. "And bandages?"

"Yes, in the upstairs bathroom. But I can get them."

"Let me," he said. "You should sit down. That's got to hurt, and you're losing a fair amount of blood." He was still pressing the paper towels to her shoulder, and his hand felt warm.

It *did* hurt, badly enough that she felt weak. She gripped the edge of the counter. "I . . . do feel a little shaky," she said.

"Come on, just sit down here." Half-turning, he reached toward the kitchen table, spun around a chair, and guided her carefully into it. He knelt in front of her.

Even in her pain she noticed that, kneeling, he was still almost her height as she sat. He took her free hand in his. "Do you feel like you're going to pass out? Do you need to put your head down for a minute?"

There was something incongruous about this tender, efficient nursing from a big man in a business suit. Esperanza smiled and shook her head. "No, I'm okay. I just got dizzy for a minute."

"Hold this against your shoulder," he instructed, lifting her hand to the paper towels stanching the flow of blood. "Put a little pressure on it. I'll get the medicine."

When he came back he soaked some paper towels in water and then pulled up a chair and sat beside her. Carefully and gently he cleaned the wound, then studied it. "I don't think you need stitches," he said.

"Of course I don't."

"But you should keep it clean and covered." As he spoke he was dabbing antibiotic cream on the wound. When he'd finished he cut a piece of gauze to fit and taped it on. "There," he said, patting her shoulder. "All set. Does it still hurt?"

She couldn't help smiling. This was a different side of Gabriel Montana. "I'm fine, Dad," she said, her voice dry. Then, seeing his eyes go flat and frozen, she realized what she'd said. It had just been an offhand comment, but it probably didn't sound that way to someone who had lost his only child. "I'm sorry," she said, grasping his hand. "I forgot that might hurt."

He shook his head and smiled quickly at her, his eyes still frozen. "That's okay."

But she was touched by the way he'd taken care of her. It had given her a glimpse into his personality. She remembered Bessie saying how, from a young age, he'd taken care of his brothers and sisters. She could imagine that he'd bandaged up any number of injuries in his day.

She understood growing up too fast, not having a childhood. And she also understood being the caretaker who never got taken care of. "No, I'm really sorry," she insisted. "I guess... you think about how your baby would have called you Dad, huh?"

He cleared his throat. "Uh-huh."

"Do you ever talk about it? Does anyone ever ask you questions?"

"Most people are afraid to," he said. "They don't want to intrude."

Was that a slam? "It would probably be more polite of me not to say anything either," she said. "I just know how it feels to keep things bottled up inside. I don't want to push, but if you want to talk sometime..."

He looked at her for a moment as if he wondered whether she was sincere. Finally he said, "I might do that sometime. I just might."

"Good. Because I really am sorry for your loss."

The ice had melted from his eyes. "Thank you. I should probably be over it by now. A lot of times, I am. For some reason, around you I get, um, emotional."

"Yeah. What's that all about? I do the same thing around you."

They were silent for a minute, during which Esperanza suddenly realized how close they were sitting together. Gabe's legs were apart, and her chair was between them; he had one arm along the back of it. It was because he'd been putting a bandage on her, but now she felt the other meanings such a semi-embrace could have. She stared at her knees.

"Well." Gabe scooted his chair back and rubbed his hands together. "We were going to talk about why you want to quit."

"Oh, right." *Because you're scaring me to death.* "I just decided I have to take the plunge with my bird business. I've been hovering on the edge of making it for almost a year now. I need to give it my full attention."

"Do you have the savings to take that risk?"

"Gabe," she reminded him, "that's not really your business."

"I know, I know. It's just that I feel somewhat responsible in your case. I think if the adoption problem hadn't come up, you wouldn't be thinking about quitting. Am I right?"

"No, that's not it."

"Then is it something to do with me?" he asked, his voice blunt.

Their eyes met, and held.

"Is it?"

"No," she said, looking down.

"You're sure?"

She nodded vigorously.

"Okay," he said. "I just don't want to be the cause of some hardship for you, even indirectly. But I *have* felt this funny kind of connection with you."

She nodded again. "Me too," she admitted, and then she could have kicked herself.

"Oh." He paused. "I'm sure I'm not really your type."

That hurt. "What do you think my type is?" she asked, lifting her head. "Some drunk in a bar, or a guy on welfare?"

"No!"

"Or do you mean I'm not your type? Isn't that what it boils down to, Gabe?"

He hesitated for a second too long. "No. Not at all."

Nodding slowly, she met his eyes. "Yes it is. I know what's going on." And because she was hurt, because she was quitting her job anyway, and because her chances of adopting a baby through this man were pretty much nil, she didn't hold back. "I've seen how you look at me, Gabe. I know you feel a little attracted. I'm not too naïve to notice the chemistry between us. But I also know we're from completely different worlds. I know you're still in love with that upper-class angel of a wife. I know you wouldn't want to be seen with the likes of me."

"That's not true, Esperanza," he said. "You make me sound like a snob."

"If the shoe fits—"

"But the shoe doesn't fit, Esperanza," he said. "Yes, we're from different worlds, and yes, I'm still struggling with some losses from the past. But I would gladly explore these feelings I have for you, if it weren't for the fact that I'm your boss."

"Uh-huh."

"I'm telling you the truth."

She spread her hands and shrugged. "It doesn't matter," she said quickly. "I'm not looking for a man." Suddenly restless, she stood up and walked over to the sink.

"Hey." He was right behind her, so close that she thought she could feel his body heat through her clothes. "I don't know what's made you think I'm holding myself above you. Quite honestly I've had a strong attraction to you almost since we met. But I don't want to be unethical by acting on it when we're in this boss-employee relationship."

A strong attraction since we met. The rush of joy she felt surprised her. Without thinking she turned around. "I'm quitting," she said, looking up at him.

"So you are." He studied her face for a moment. Then he put his arms on her shoulders. When she kept looking at him, he bent down and kissed her once, lightly, then lifted his head. "It's like striking a match," he said, his voice rough as gravel. "Feel this." He took her hand and pressed it against his chest, and she felt the pounding of his heart.

"Mine, too," she whispered.

He took a couple of deep breaths and then something like consternation crossed his face. "I'm sorry."

"It's okay," she said and reached up to stroke his cheek, rough like sandpaper.

"No, it's really not okay," he said. "I shouldn't have done that. I don't know what I was thinking."

"Don't worry about it." She leaned against his chest. His arms tightened around her and he rested a cheek on top of her head. Maybe it was *because* he was so worried, so careful to do the right thing, so surprised that he hadn't been the perfect professional, that she herself felt comfortable with what had happened, with that light, emotional kiss. She didn't feel like she had to draw the line with Gabe, nor fight him off. In fact, she felt warm and safe in his arms.

But it was different for him. She felt it in the way he carefully put her away from him, saw it in the guarded expression on his face. "I'd better go," he said. "Esperanza, again, I'm sorry. That was inexcusable."

"Hey, you're excused, okay? It's not like you attacked me. It was a kiss. And not even much of one."

"Still, I should have had more control," he said, almost to himself.

"Heaven help us if you get any more control than you already have." But she wondered if the issue of professionalism was all he was worried about. Most men she'd known wouldn't even have cared about that. Maybe his regret had to do with who she was. Or maybe he felt like he'd betrayed his dead wife.

That thought wiped away the last remnants of her warm desire. "I'll see you at work," she said, following him toward the front door, handing him his coat.

"Right. At work." He shook his head and walked out the door, muttering something under his breath. It sounded like, "and only at work."

Maybe, and maybe not.

6

When Gabe heard a car door slam outside his mother's house the next Sunday, he looked around the crowded room. "Wonder who that is?" he said to his sister Bianca. "I thought everyone was already here."

"Probably Esperanza," she said.

"What?" he said in an unintentionally loud voice. Then, more quietly, "You invited her?"

"You knew I was going to, didn't you? I said something about it last week."

"I forgot." More like he'd tried to block it out of his mind, along with any other thoughts related to Esperanza. Ever since that evening at her house, he had been kicking himself for kissing her, and looking for ways to avoid her. At work, he had stayed in his office as much as possible when she was there.

But thoughts of how tiny and delicate she had felt in his arms had invaded his mind at all kinds of inappropriate moments. When he was working out. When he stayed late at the office to do his paperwork.

When he tried to go to sleep at night.

But he felt ashamed. Even though he should have known better, he had let himself get carried away. He was so attracted to her that he had ignored the fact that she worked for him, and that he wasn't interested in getting involved with anyone.

It was his job to take care of the people at the agency, and he'd fallen short.

Restlessly Gabe went to the window and looked out. Sure enough, it was Esperanza, pulling something out of her little car's back seat. Even in jeans and a simple red turtleneck, she looked too good to him.

He let the curtain drop and started to walk toward the basement door.

"Where are *you* going?" Bianca asked in a low voice as he passed her.

"Mom wanted me to pull out the Christmas decorations," he said.

"Aren't you going to say hi to Esperanza first?"

"I'll catch her later."

"Don't be rude. She's shy, and she's coming into a house full of strangers."

"Whose fault is that?" Gabe asked irritably.

The doorbell rang. "Ask yourself why you're so cranky," Bianca advised him in a whisper as she headed for the door.

When Esperanza came in, the whole room seemed to buzz slightly, as if electrically charged. Not that she was wildly dramatic; in fact, she was just talking quietly to Bianca, and then being introduced to their brother John and his two children. But he couldn't take his eyes off her shiny black hair and warm smile.

Esperanza acknowledged him with a little wave, but didn't speak to him, possibly because he hung back and didn't go up to her. Then John introduced Nicola, their other sister.

Gabe felt an urge to protect Esperanza as soon as he saw

Nicki's stiff, social smile. Nicki had been Melissa's closest friend, and she didn't approve of Gabe dating anyone else. Although she had her good side, she was the most like their mother in her brittle personality and strong opinions.

Esperanza held out her free hand to Nicki, but Nicki pretended not to see it.

"What an interesting looking—what is that, a bucket of dirt?" Nicki's voice held snobbish condemnation.

"Actually, it's a cake," Esperanza said. "And I'm sure glad there are some kids here. Otherwise, I'd feel really silly for bringing a cake like this."

"Is it a cake for kids?" one of Nicki's four-year-old twins piped up.

"Uh-huh. Look." Esperanza squatted down and pulled the plastic wrap off the bucket she carried.

"It looks like dirt!" the other twin said.

"I know, but we're going to eat it!" Esperanza explained, smiling at them.

"I'm not eating that! There's *worms* on it!"

"What *is* it?" Nicki asked.

"It's a dirt cake," Esperanza explained, standing up. "Haven't you ever seen one?"

"No, I'm afraid I haven't."

"Can we try some?"

"Please, *Mom*, just a little?"

"Maybe after dinner," Nicki said grudgingly.

Bianca had reappeared and was peering into the bucket. "Gads, that does look like dirt," she said. "What is it really?"

"Crushed up oreos, mixed with some whipped cream. And those are candy worms," Esperanza explained. "It's really good. We just happened to have all the stuff for it."

"Cool. It's obviously a hit. Come meet Mom. Oh, and there's Gabe, but you already know him."

Esperanza glanced at Gabe as she and Bianca walked past. There was something quizzical in her expression and something knowing too. He wondered if she had noticed his avoidance of her, and suddenly he felt ashamed.

He should be direct with her. They should probably talk out what had happened. Then they could chalk it up to chemistry and get back to being distant colleagues. Or acquaintances, since Esperanza would only be at the agency for one more week.

He stood and went to the kitchen where Bianca had taken Esperanza. There, their mother stood at the kitchen counter peeling potatoes. While everyone else had changed into casual clothes, she still wore her church dress, stockings, and heels, with an apron tied over them. That was his mother. Formal even at home.

He hadn't heard the introductions, but Mom was being guardedly friendly, which was good. She was so moody that sometimes she was unintentionally cool with their friends. It had always been that way, and while the family was accustomed to it, outsiders were sometimes put off.

Gabe walked in, turned around one of the chairs at the kitchen table, and sat down, leaning on it, just wanting to listen. He had to admit that he liked a kitchen with women in it. The black-and-chrome of his condo's kitchen looked stylish, but this place sounded and smelled like home.

"Do you need any help with those potatoes?" Esperanza was asking. "I'm a pretty good peeler."

"Well, thank you. If you wouldn't mind, then I could check on the roast."

"And no way am I cooking," Bianca said. "I'll do anything else, but working in a café makes you hate cooking on your days off."

"I like to cook," Esperanza said. "But it seems silly to cook up a lot of stuff for just one person." She took the knife from Gabe's mother and started peeling potatoes in neat spirals.

"Did you come from a big family, dear?"

There was the briefest of pauses. Just enough to make Gabe realize how awkward it must be to always have to explain your upbringing.

"Sometimes," Esperanza said finally. "I was raised in a few different foster homes, so there were usually at least five or six other kids there. In one house, there were ten kids."

"Oh, my." Gabe's mother paused at the refrigerator door, frowning. "That seems a bit much. Why couldn't your own family take care of you?"

Gabe and Bianca shot each other quick glances. Gabe desperately wanted to say something but he couldn't think of what would help.

"Actually," Esperanza said, without a pause in her peeling, "I don't know anything about my biological family, except things like my mother's blood type from some forms one of my foster families got from the agency. I don't know what their situation was."

"Probably a single mother." Gabe's mother turned away and slid a casserole dish into the oven.

"Mom, could you show me those new towels you bought me?" Bianca said.

As the two of them left, Bianca nodded toward Esperanza, frowning. Gabe knew exactly what she meant. *Go repair the damage Mom did.* It was a message they sent each other frequently.

Esperanza was still peeling potatoes, and Gabe went to her immediately. Touching her shoulder lightly, he said, "I'm sorry my mother was rude."

"No big deal," she said. "People ask questions like that all the time."

"It doesn't hurt your feelings?"

She shook her head. "Can't let it. I had to develop a pretty thick skin, growing up as a foster child. You can't let people's comments bother you."

"Oh." He pushed himself up to sit on the counter beside her. "I want you to feel welcome."

"That's funny," she said, looking up from her work for the first time. "I had the impression you wished I would go away."

"I . . ." Gabe got lost in those dark eyes for a minute, and then he shook his head. "It's not that I want you to go away. It's that I don't want to give you the wrong idea."

"Which is?"

"Which is . . . that something is going to happen between us."

"Oh." She went back to peeling potatoes.

It felt awkward that she was ignoring him. "How's your arm?" he asked finally.

Esperanza shook the water off her hand and pushed up her sleeve to reveal the wound she'd gotten from Paco last week.

"Let me see." Gabe scooted closer and lifted her arm to inspect the wound. "It's healing well." Her arm was so tiny.

"I had a good doctor."

He still had hold of her arm, and their gazes were locked.

"Careful," she said finally, pulling away, her eyes never leaving his. "You might give me the wrong idea."

"Gabriel!" His mother's voice brought him back to reality. "Are you helping with the cooking?"

"That would be a first." Bianca came into the kitchen behind their mother. And then everyone else came in and the conversation grew general as everyone pitched in to get the meal on the table.

Dinner felt uncomfortable to Gabe. He was so conscious of Esperanza that he couldn't eat as heartily as he usually did, which drew comment from his brother and sisters. His mother kept bringing up Melissa, whom she'd adored; it was obvious that she was warning off Esperanza after that suspiciously-romantic scene she had walked in on in the kitchen.

Esperanza didn't seem shaken by any of it, though. She talked to Bianca, their brother John, Nicola's husband Lonnie, and the children, and ignored the little barbs of Nicola and their mother. She helped with the cleanup after dinner. And then she joined the men in the den to watch part of a football game, and impressed John and Lonnie by having an informed opinion about the referee's calls.

In the middle of the afternoon, when she announced that she was leaving, Gabe walked out to her car with her. "I'm sorry if the family scene was a little intense," he said. "I'm used to it, but it must seem weird from the outside."

"I liked it," Esperanza said. "It's a treat to hang around a big family who gets along."

"Well, we don't always get along. I thought people were a little snippy today."

"If people don't throw ashtrays and beer bottles at each other, I consider it pretty peaceful," she said.

Gabe frowned. "Was it really that rough the way you grew up?"

"Sure. I wasn't very lucky in my placements. There are a lot of good foster families, but I didn't happen to end up with them."

"How'd you turn out so together?"

Esperanza raised her eyebrows. "So you think I'm together, do you?"

"Well, for someone with that background, yes. I think it would leave some scars."

"It did. But I do okay."

She shivered, and Gabe took her hands in his. "It's a cold day," he said. "You should be wearing gloves."

"Uh-huh." She pulled away. "See you later."

To Gabe, her departure seemed a little hasty. He stood watching the taillights of her small car disappear in the darkening afternoon. Only when he couldn't see any more signs of Esperanza did he realize he was standing in 20-degree weather without a coat. He turned and walked back into the house.

~

LATER THAT NIGHT, Gabe looked around his apartment as if with new eyes. He counted eight pictures of Melissa and their child in the living room alone.

He picked up his favorite photograph and studied it. Melissa was lying back in the fall leaves, laughing as she held little Kaylene above her.

They had both been killed the next week.

If only they hadn't chosen that out-of-the-way Mexican beach town for their vacation. If only they hadn't gone for a stroll on the boardwalk at the same time as some drug dealing punks.

If only he'd noticed that the truck driving toward them had the barrel of a gun sticking out the window. If only he hadn't hung back, while Melissa walked ahead with Kaylene, to give some quarters and chewing gum to a couple of begging street kids...

But none of those "if onlys" had happened. His wife and child had gotten in the way of some drug lord's quest for revenge. They were gone. There was never going to be justice or retribution.

"Hey Angel," he said softly. "Bianca tells me I ought to move on with my life."

In the picture, Melissa's laughing face didn't change.

"I'm lonely," he admitted. "I need some companionship."

He thought about what Melissa might have said, how she'd tried to fix up their friends, how she wanted everyone to have the happiness she and Gabe had found in marriage.

She wouldn't have wanted him to live alone the rest of his life. And with her generosity of spirit, she wouldn't have been jealous about his finding someone else, if she herself could no longer be his wife.

He put the picture back down on the entertainment center, where it had always been.

Then he walked around the room, picking up the other seven framed photos, and stacked them on the counter that separated the kitchen from the dining area. Walked into the bedroom and gathered up three more. Two from the kitchen.

Gabe rooted around in his storage closet until he found a box big enough to hold the collection. Carefully, he wrapped each framed photograph and put them into the box separating them with newspaper. He found some packing tape and taped the box closed. On the outside he wrote "pictures" and the years they covered.

In the basement of the condominium complex was a group of storage bins for the residents. In Gabe's cubbyhole were his skis, his bike, a small gas grill, and a couple of computer boxes.

He found a safe corner for the pictures, putting them on top of another box so that if the basement should flood, the pictures would be safe. Carefully he locked the storage bin behind him.

Back upstairs, he flipped on the television, then flipped it off. He opened his refrigerator and surveyed the slim pickings there, then closed it again.

He stood with his hand on the phone for at least five minutes. He should do something. He should call Esperanza, ask her out to a movie.

It would be okay with Melissa.

Instead, he called into the office to let them know he was taking a personal day. and then got into bed. When he got up, a full twelve hours later, he went for a long, hard run.

Took a visit to the cemetery.

And, yeah, cried.

And *then* he picked the phone up, dialed Esperanza's number, and talked her into going to a movie with him.

7

Almost three weeks later, at a crowded outdoor ice rink, Esperanza clung to Gabe's arm and took a few awkward steps, her ankles wobbling. The cold air and the challenge almost made her forget the slight breathlessness she felt every time they were together.

Almost, but not quite.

"Haven't you ever skated before?" Gabe sounded both amused and surprised.

"No. But I always wanted to. We used to watch the skaters when I was a teenager." Losing her concentration, she windmilled her arm madly as her skates skidded underneath her.

Gabe tried to catch her, but lost his balance himself, and a second later they were both on the ice, Esperanza half on top of Gabe.

"Hey, you're supposed to help me, not fall down too," she gasped.

"I didn't know I was dealing with a total beginner." He ran his hands down her arms, squeezing her wrists gently. "Are you okay? Do you hurt anywhere?"

She shook her head, suddenly even more breathless. "I feel okay."

"Me, too." He leaned a little closer and their frosty breath mingled in the cool air.

"Hey, get outta the way." The flat, irritated voice brought them back to reality. They had driven into Cleveland to have a good pizza dinner, and on the way had decided to stop for a little skating. It was their third date in two weeks.

They scrambled to their feet, and Gabe helped Esperanza make two awkward circuits around the pond.

"It looked easier from outside the fence," she complained, her breathing rough, her ankles aching.

"Want to rest a few minutes?"

She nodded, and he led her to a bench. Getting off the skates felt heavenly. She stretched out her legs in front of her. "You seem pretty comfortable skating, unlike me."

"It's fun. I used to come here pretty often."

"With Melissa?" she guessed.

He hesitated, and then nodded.

So that was why he'd been acting a little nervous. Good. She had thought it was because he knew something about this neighborhood, something about her past. "Does it make you sad, being here?"

"Not really. I'm enjoying teaching you."

"Well, this skating student is tired. You go on. Show me how it's done while I rest."

So Gabe skated off. Hands clasped behind his back, he moved with strong, smooth thrusts of his jean-clad legs, then glided in long, graceful arcs around the pond.

Esperanza sighed. She could just imagine Gabe and the beautiful, blond Melissa skating beautifully together, making it all seem effortless. She had watched couples like that as she had walked past this park on her way home from high school or her part-time job as a waitress.

Tiny tendrils of self-deprecation curled around the edges of her mind. She would never catch up to Gabe, never reach his education level, never share the advantages he'd had. The way they had skated together—her stumbling and falling, sometimes pulling him down with her—was just the way this relationship they were starting on was destined to go.

But thinking like that brought the automatic rebuttal she'd perfected after years of practice. Although she hadn't had his education or advantages, she had had plenty of life experiences, and learning from them had given her strength and determination. And she was God's workmanship, as this morning's devotional had emphasized.

She stood and made her way to a less-travelled part of the pond, pushing off and gliding the way Gabe had showed her, only more slowly.

Half-an-hour later, bruised from several falls, she felt confident enough to move back into the mainstream of the pond, and when Gabe skated up beside her she smiled victoriously at him. "Look! I'm getting better!"

"You look great," he said, his deep brown eyes pinned on her. "I don't think I've ever seen anyone improve so quickly."

"I fell about five or six times," she admitted, taking the arm he offered.

"I saw. I also saw you get right back up again. You're pretty determined."

She nodded. "That's one thing I am."

They took several more circuits of the pond. The air was crisp, and the surrounding snow muffled the shouts and laughter of the other skaters. Occasionally they caught the aroma of hot dogs and mulled cider from a food stand next to the skate-rental hutch.

The third time they passed the food stand, Esperanza slowed down, dragging her toe as Gabe had taught her. "I'm starved," she said. "What about you?"

He nodded. "Only not for hot dogs. I still want pizza."

So they turned in their skates and headed down the busy urban street toward Mama Cippo's Italian Restaurant.

"Did you and Melissa go to this restaurant too?" she asked.

Gabe shook his head. "She was afraid of this neighborhood," he said. "The skating pond was as far as she'd go."

"And you're not afraid?"

"No. My frat brothers and I went to Mama C's all the time. Best pizza in Cleveland. Even better than the places in Little Italy." He hesitated. "I . . . assumed you wouldn't mind the neighborhood, but if you'd rather go someplace a little more upscale, we could do that."

She shook her head. "No, I always wanted to try Mama C's." She didn't tell him that it had been out of her reach, growing up, that she could count on one hand the number of times any of her foster families had gone to a sit-down restaurant.

"Do you mind walking? If you're tired from skating, we could drive."

"No." It wasn't likely that anyone she feared still hung around this neighborhood anyway. Wayne was out of state and his cronies should have moved on, too. "I'm fine. I'd like to walk."

So they headed down eleventh street.

"You said you used to watch the skaters," Gabe said as they sidled past a newspaper stand. "So you lived around here?"

Esperanza nodded. "When Rhonda and I got moved from Hopewell Corners, this was where we came to live." She gestured vaguely to the left. "A couple of blocks over that way."

"Rough neighborhood," Gabe commented.

"By some people's standards, it was," she agreed. "But just

like in most neighborhoods, there are good folks and bad ones. I made friends."

"You seem pretty resilient. It's one thing I admire about you."

Esperanza felt her cheeks heating up. "I never thought I'd go out with a guy who used two-dollar words like 'resilient,' that's for sure," she joked.

He laughed and draped an arm lightly across her shoulders. "I never thought I'd date a woman who *was* resilient, but I like it."

Esperanza's breath caught. Walking with Gabe beside her, the old neighborhood truly felt safe. *She* felt safe. Warm. Almost ... loved. She snaked an arm around his waist, and he pulled her slightly closer to him.

"Well, well. Look who's here."

The voice carried above the street noises, coming from the doorway of a bar. Esperanza froze. A sick shiver moved from her head to her toes and back again, settling in her stomach. She wanted to keep walking, even to run, but Gabe had slowed at the sight of the man who detached himself from a small crowd emerging from the tavern door, smiling at them.

Waster Wayne. Wayne the Brain. Wayne the Psycho.

Wayne, the foster brother who'd tried to molest both her and Rhonda repeatedly, had almost succeeded, and had left them both with scars they'd never lose.

"Es-per-anza A-cos-ta!" He drew out her name in the same fake Spanish accent he'd found amusing years ago. "I thought you were far, far away from Locust Street. And here you are back in the old neighborhood."

She couldn't answer. She just stood stiff, cautious, ready to flee.

"Don't you have a hug for your old foster brother?" His voice was sarcastic, knowing.

She took a step back. "I have a bad cold," she lied quickly, remembering Wayne's dislike of being sick, "so you'd better keep your distance." She took deep breaths, her mind racing. She just had to keep him from finding out where she lived, and it would be okay.

He stopped, crossing his arms over her chest, and studied her. "You don't look sick."

"Oh, but I am. It's terrible." She glanced up at Gabe, who stood beside her, a slight frown on his face, and blessed his size and build. "Gabe, this is Wayne Little. Wayne, Gabriel Montana."

Gabe held out his right hand to Wayne without taking his other arm from around her shoulders. It was as if he sensed that she needed his strength.

"You live in the city now?" Wayne asked them casually.

"No," they both said at the same time, and Esperanza tightened her arm around Gabe's waist, warning him to silence. "We live way up north," she lied. "We're just in town for a little pizza and shopping."

"You married?" Wayne asked.

"No . . . not yet," Esperanza said, forcing a coy laugh and willing Gabe not to betray the fact that they'd barely started dating.

To his credit, he caught on. "We've been shopping for rings," he said in a hearty, man-to-man voice. "I knew I'd better let her pick out what she wanted."

"Oh." Wayne's voice was flat.

Fortunately, his buddies from the bar had decided on their next stop. "C'mon, Little, we're going to Frankie's," someone called.

Esperanza watched Wayne with the observational skills that she'd developed after two years of living with him, of defending herself from him. She saw him ponder staying, finding out more about her. She saw his quick, assessing glance at Gabe. And she saw him decide to let it go.

"Later," he said to them, and Esperanza let out the breath she'd been holding.

"Later," she breathed, and Gabe said, "nice to meet you."

As they headed on down the block, Esperanza's heart pounded and she took long, slow, calming breaths. Wayne Little. Right here, large as life. She shuddered.

Gabe didn't speak for several moments, but he kept his arm tight around her, and she was grateful for its support. After a few minutes, he slowed. "Here's Mama C's."

Esperanza walked through the wooden doorway, stood numbly in the crowded, steamy foyer while Mama C checked for a table, and then followed the large woman to a booth near the kitchen. She slid in and stared at the red-and-white vinyl tablecloth while Gabe, across from her, put in an order for two glasses of the house red wine.

Wayne wasn't in California. Wayne lived right here. Her stomach churned.

"Hey." Gabe reached across the table and touched her hand. "What was that all about?"

She looked at the tablecloth again, counting squares. Then she met his eyes. "That was a kid who lived in the house with Rhonda and me, and some younger kids, when we were teenagers. He was the biological son of the foster parents."

Gabe nodded, waiting, his eyes sad.

"He . . . was a bully. *Is* a bully. That's why I didn't want him to know where I was living." She frowned. "I thought he was settled out west."

"Is that why you wanted him to think we were engaged?"

She let her breath out in a sigh that sounded too much like a sob. "Yeah. I'm sorry about that, Gabe. I just thought . . . I mean, he seemed to be making that assumption anyway, so it seemed like I might as well go along with it. If he thinks I've got a defensive lineman in my life, it might make him think twice about harassing me. He doesn't have to know we're just dating casually."

Gabe cleared his throat. "I'm not much for casual dating anyway," he said, "and my relationship with you feels a lot more than casual."

Before she could interpret that little bombshell, their wine came, and Esperanza took a grateful gulp, then coughed at the unexpectedly strong taste. She grabbed a napkin, grimacing.

"Are you okay?"

Esperanza felt a wry smile turn up the corners of her mouth. "You're going to regret asking me out. First, I make you fall down, skating. Then I use you to defend me against my obnoxious former housemates. And then you find out I never even drink wine." She threw up her hands dramatically. "There goes the sophisticated impression I was trying to make."

Gabe shook his head. "You don't have to make an impression for me," he said. "I like you the way you are. A lot." He closed one of his large hands over hers, completely enveloping it.

The warmth spread from her hand up her arm, a slow burning. As he gently fondled her hand, she felt her breath catch, and she met his eyes to find him watching her closely. Her cheeks burned and she pulled her hand away.

He was silent for a moment. "Eppie, I want to ask you something," he said finally. "I've noticed that you have a little bit of . . . physical shyness around men. Around me, at least."

She stared at him. "You think I'm shy around you?" And she'd felt she was making such progress, letting him hold her hand or put his arm around her, not flinching away.

He was nodding. "Not always. But I've noticed that you can freeze up when we start to get, well, close."

"That's putting it kind of strongly, isn't it? I mean, I know I haven't fallen into bed with you, but we haven't known each other all that long—"

"I didn't mean you should," he said, holding up a hand. "I'm just asking about something I noticed."

Esperanza waited while the pizza they'd ordered was placed on their table, and the waitress had put a piece on each plate. The rich smell of pepperoni and melted cheese wafted up, but she didn't feel hungry anymore. "If you don't like going out with me, why do you keep calling?"

Gabe stared at her, a bite of pizza hovering halfway to his mouth. "Did I say I didn't like going out with you?"

"No, but who wants to date an icicle?"

"Someone who likes a challenge," he said, grinning at her.

She rolled her eyes and started picking at the pizza with her fork. "I'm not a football opponent, Gabe. Maybe I haven't had much experience with men. Maybe I'm even a little uptight. That's who I am, and if you don't like it, leave me alone."

"Is it because of Wayne?"

Esperanza put her fork down very carefully, thinking. She never, ever told anyone about the worst incident with Wayne, and she wasn't about to start with Gabriel Montana. However nice he was, however strong and protective and kind, he wouldn't understand that she had *had* to fight back. And he wouldn't understand a court system that had put her away for it. To Gabe's type, the court was a friend.

"I'm sorry. If you don't want to talk about it—"

She shrugged, avoiding his eyes. "It's okay. It's because of Wayne, and guys like him. You end up fighting off a lot of creeps in neighborhoods like this. And in the foster care system, unless you're lucky enough to get a good long-term placement."

"So men are a threat?"

"Sort of," she said, grateful that he'd gotten off the specific track of Wayne. "I was lucky. I learned how to be tough at a young age. It's just hard to turn it off, I guess."

He nodded. "I'm sorry you had to deal with that," he said, his voice sincere. "And if there's any way I can help you protect yourself now, you can count on me."

"I was glad you were with me when I saw Wayne."

After a few minutes of quiet eating, Esperanza decided that if Gabe could ask her tough questions about her past, then she could do the same to him. "So," she said, "if it's not too hard to talk about, can you tell me about what happened to Melissa? And the baby?"

Gabe hesitated and then put down the piece of pizza he'd been eating. He looked off into the smoky darkness of the restaurant. "There's not much to tell," he said, his voice flat. "We were vacationing in Mexico, walking on the boardwalk. Unfortunately, so were some drug traffickers, and . . . Melissa and the baby got caught in the middle."

"You saw it happen?" Esperanza asked, horrified.

He nodded. "I'd stopped to give some change to some street kids. They were dirty, sick, you know, so Melissa had walked on with the baby. Right into the crossfire."

"And there was nothing you could do."

A muscle under his eye started twitching, and she wished she could take the question back. But he plowed on, telling the story in a detached, dead voice. "I saw her go down, and the stroller was rolling ahead. I ran toward it, but I caught a bullet myself. Those automatic weapons, you know . . . by the time I could get to her, Kaylene was shot, too. Along with the guys they'd been aiming for. They hit their target, and then some."

"Oh, Gabe." She touched his hand, squeezed it gently. "I'm so sorry. How awful for you."

A humorless smile crossed his face. "Not so bad for me. I survived."

"And you feel guilty about that?"

He looked surprised. Slowly, he nodded. "You bet I do. I should have been able to protect my family."

"Against random violence? You're not a superhero."

"The thing is," he said slowly, "Melissa was nervous, being in a foreign country for the first time. She practically clung to me the whole week. The only reason she wasn't right by my side was those street kids. If I hadn't stopped—"

"You can't beat yourself up for wanting to help kids," she said. "It's a part of who you are. It was just bad luck, Gabe. The world can be a really rotten place, and you and Melissa got caught in that."

His eyes were closed. "And then when I dove for the baby, that's when she was killed. Maybe if I hadn't called attention to myself, they would have driven on without that last round of gunfire."

Esperanza's heart twisted in her chest. She gripped both of his hands in hers. "Look at me, Gabe," she said, and waited until he opened his eyes. "You have to stop that. You can't change anything in the past, and you'll go crazy if you keep reliving it. You have to do the best you can with each day. You had rotten luck, and it wasn't fair, but it wasn't your fault."

"I wish that could sink in," he said.

Mama C came to their table then. "You don't like the pizza?" she asked in an accusatory tone.

"No, I mean, yes," Esperanza said because Gabe didn't look exactly ready to shoot the breeze with a stranger. "It was great. But I guess we ordered too much."

"You take it home, stay out of the kitchen tomorrow. Okay?"

"Sure, we'd love to take it home."

Their drive back to Hopewell Corners was quiet. Esperanza felt drained, both from the encounter with Wayne and from learning about the distressing history of Gabe's loss. Looking at his face, which for the first time since she'd met him seemed to sag slightly, she assumed he felt the same.

When they arrived at her house he turned off the engine and sat still.

"I'd invite you in," she said, "but it's late. Besides, I wouldn't want to ruin my icicle image."

He looked at her then, a weary smile on his face. "You learned some pretty ugly things about me tonight," he said.

"Some *sad* things," she corrected. "It wasn't your fault, Gabe. You must know that."

He nodded without speaking.

"And you learned some ugly things about my past, too," she said. "I guess neither of us has had things simple."

He turned to her then, and held out his arms. When she moved into them, the embrace felt different. It was more comfort than heat; it was shelter from a world that had treated them both harshly. It lasted a long time.

When he finally loosened his grip and looked into her eyes, his were warm and just the slightest bit shiny, as if with tears. Then she thought she must have been seeing things, because he kissed her with all the tender persuasion in the world. And that lasted a long time too.

8

"I'm not dating him just so I can adopt a baby!"

"Well, then, why are you, Miss *I don't need anybody* Acosta?" Rhonda's voice, loud over the sound of the radio, was like a wave of conscience gone bad.

"I don't know!" Esperanza twitched her fingers through her wet, tangled hair and started combing it. She was getting ready for another date with Gabe, and she was wondering the same thing Rhonda was. Time for a change of subject. "Hey, didn't you say Maria was going to come visit?"

"Maria... " Rhonda's face was blank.

"Our little foster sister?"

"Oh, yeah. She texted. Her baby got sick, and her husband's working overtime, so she said it might not be until after the holidays."

"You could've told me!" Esperanza mock-scolded.

"I'm a little scattered with the new job and all. Sorry."

"It's just, I can't wait to see her." She'd felt a special kinship with the girl, not only because of their shared victimhood, but because of Maria's similar Latina coloring. At times, during the year they'd lived under the same roof, she'd pretended Maria was her real little sister.

"And don't think I didn't notice you changed the subject." Rhonda headed out of Esperanza's room and into her own. "You ought to think about Gabe and what you're doing with him."

Since their skating date, they had gone out several more times. Esperanza felt closer to Gabe after their emotional conversation that night, and she trusted him more. It was natural, she guessed, that their attraction to one another would grow too. Each time, he had kissed her lightly, but hadn't tried to do more. She supposed it was reverse psychology; she found herself *wanting* to cling to him, wanting more physical contact.

But she didn't want to get serious with a man. So for this date, she'd tried to find a little safeguard against too much romance: she was taking Tanisha with them when they went to the Light-Up Night at the city zoo. That would keep their stroll through the holiday darkness from turning into a big romantic opportunity.

Rhonda stuck her head around the corner. "Tanisha's on the phone," she said, handing Esperanza her cell phone.

Esperanza answered, following Rhonda down the stairs. Tanisha could still come, but had to be home early, and wondered if she could bring her friend. When she ended the call, Rhonda was leaning back against the kitchen counter, arms crossed over her chest. "Well?" Rhonda said.

"Well, what? Tanisha's bringing another little girl."

Rhonda shrugged. "More chance for you and Gabe to talk, if Tanisha is busy with her friend."

"I know. That's what I'm worried about."

"Aw, why be worried? Enjoy it."

Esperanza shook her head. "You know me. I'm just not that relaxed about men."

"Yeah, but look. You want to adopt a baby like nothing else. And they told you at the agency that the only way you'll get chosen is if you have a husband."

Rhonda's voice echoed a tiny voice that had gone through Esperanza's own head, and she gave the reply she'd instantly given to herself. "That would be using him. I would never marry someone unless I loved him and wanted to marry him. It would be wrong."

"Yeah, well, I guess I don't see it that way. If he's getting what he wants, and you're getting what you want, who says it has to be exactly the same thing?"

"What do you mean?" Esperanza asked uneasily.

"Look. He gets what all men want, which, knowing you, he's not going to get *unless* he marries you. And you get a baby. Sounds like an even trade."

"Forget it, Rhonda. Marriage is a sacred contract. It's not a deal."

~

Two hours later, as she strolled through the lighted zoo hand in hand with Gabe, Esperanza tried to push Rhonda's words out of her mind.

She wasn't going to marry Gabe. For Pete's sake, they had just started dating. Going out on a few dates had nothing to do with marriage; most people did it all the time, without taking it seriously.

But most people weren't her. Or Gabe. And this scene was getting so romantic.

Gabe, sensitive to her interests, headed first for the birds, and they spent a long time looking at the beautiful creatures. Then they followed Tanisha's request and strolled through the areas of the big cats. There were other people there, but as if in respect for the season and the night, people talked quietly, even children.

When Tanisha and her friend, Andraya, got too cold, they all went into one of the pavilions for hot chocolate.

"What do you want for Christmas?" Gabe asked Tanisha after they'd settled at a table near the window, where they could look out at the lights.

"Want my Mama to come for me," Tanisha said.

"Your mama ain't coming," Andraya scoffed.

"She is, too. I had me a dream." And Tanisha launched into a colorful description of a dream in which her mother had appeared in a big white limousine, rich and famous, and whisked Tanisha off to her Hollywood mansion to live in luxury.

"Yeah, well that's a nice story," Andraya said.

"It is," Gabe agreed, to Esperanza's surprise. "You should write it down."

"Write it down?" Tanisha asked. "Like a letter to Santa Claus?"

"Uh-huh. Or like a story, or a poem. Did your teacher ever ask you to write a story?"

"It ain't just a story!" Tanisha cried out, her eyes suddenly shining with tears. She stood up quickly.

Esperanza wrapped her arms around the little girl before she could run off. "He didn't mean it wasn't true, just that it was a good story," she said quietly. "True things can be stories too, you know."

Tanisha cuddled in her lap, her thumb going to her mouth even though she was eight years old. "My mama coming," she muttered stubbornly.

"Okay," Esperanza said, rocking her a little. That longing for a real mother echoed an ache that had hummed through Esperanza's entire childhood like sad background music. She stroked Tanisha's braids gently, rhythmically.

Around them, a few people stared at the sight of a girl of Tanisha's age being cuddled like a small child. Gabe looked distressed, and Andraya opened her mouth, probably to make some cutting remark.

"I have an idea," Esperanza said quickly. "In the zoo's gift shop, I think there were some books that were true stories. Gabe, do you think you could pick out a couple of them for me?"

"Sure." Gabe said, looking relieved. "Want to help?" he asked Andraya.

She agreed, and together they hurried off to do the assigned task.

By the time they returned, Tanisha was calmer and ready to look at the books. And a little while later, she was ready to go home.

After they dropped the girls off, Gabe invited Esperanza to his house for coffee and Christmas cookies baked by his mother and sister. She hesitated, torn between wanting the evening to continue and fearing what might happen with Gabe.

He had started up the truck and was driving slowly along the street toward her house, which they would pass if they continued on to his place.

"Well, what do you think?" he asked. "Do you want to come over, or not?"

"I . . . well, maybe. I don't know."

He reached over and covered her hand with his. "You can't use getting up early for work as an excuse now," he said.

"Hey, birds get up early. I'm as busy with building my business as I was working for Open Arms, probably more."

"Then just agree to hang out with me for a while," he said. "My place feels lonelier and lonelier. I'd like the company."

When he put it like that, what could she say? "Okay. But only for a little while."

Ten minutes later, after rattling around his kitchen, Gabe joined her in the living room. "Coffee will be ready in a couple of minutes," he said.

"Are you lonelier here because you took down the pictures of your wife?" she asked.

"You noticed." He sounded surprised.

"Uh-huh. The last time I was here, it was like a museum. Now it looks more..."

"More what? Normal?"

"Well, sort of. Actually, it looks a little empty."

"What do you mean?" Gabe looked around the room. "Not decorated right?"

"It's *decorated*," she said, "but I'm not sure if I see *you* here."

"Not my forte." He shrugged. "I'm a guy. I don't really know how to make it a home. Now, your place, that seems like a home."

Esperanza laughed. "It's definitely lived-in. Rhonda makes sure of that. There's always nail polish sitting out, and magazines, and shoes." A wave of sadness passed over her as she remembered how messy it had been just a few weeks earlier. "It's nothing like when the twins were there."

"You still miss them?"

"Yeah."

Gabe stretched an arm along the top of the couch. Gently he stroked Esperanza's hair, just a couple of strokes. "You're good with kids," he said. "You really saved the situation with Tanisha tonight."

His praised warmed her even as she tried to shrug it off. "Thanks for the compliment, but with a child like that, it's always touch and go. Who knew she'd get so upset?"

"I felt bad to hurt her feelings. But that story about her mom coming back was such an obvious fantasy."

Esperanza nodded. "But it's a fantasy she needs to hold on to."

"Doesn't it keep her from living in the present?"

"Her present-day reality isn't that great," Esperanza explained. "Her foster mom sometimes threatens to send her away. There's not a lot of attention at that house. You may not have known it, but this night out at the zoo was probably the highlight of her Christmas season."

Gabe blew out a sigh. "I wish we could do something about that, but there's such a shortage of safe foster homes. So many kids in need." They sat for a moment, and then he spoke again. "Anyway, I think you do a good job with kids. I'd like to see your dream about adopting a baby come true."

Esperanza's heart twisted. "Taking care of Tanisha makes me want it even more," she admitted. "It really hurts to think it might not happen."

"I think the coffee's probably ready," Gabe said and stood up in a hurry, hitting his knee against the coffee table.

Esperanza spent the couple of minutes he was gone feeling anxious. Gabe was acting strange. Had she made him uncomfortable by talking about her continuing desire to adopt a baby? But he had brought it up.

And then Rhonda's discussion of where their dating might lead came back to the forefront of her mind, and she realized she'd been thinking about it all evening on some level. Was Gabe acting jumpy because he wanted to deepen the relationship?

But what if he just wanted sex? Not only did she think it would be wrong, she also worried about her own inhibitions. The idea that always kicked up in her mind was that men with physical love on their mind were animals, to be fought off. Although intellectually she knew that sex within marriage could be an important bond, physically her body reacted against such closeness.

So why was she sitting in a man's apartment at nine in the evening? Why wasn't she at home in her flannel nightgown, binge-watching sitcoms with Rhonda?

Just as she stood up, Gabe came back into the room. He was carrying two mugs of coffee, and under his arm he clenched a tin of cookies and some napkins. "I hope you weren't counting on milk or cream," he said, "because I'm flat out. I always drink coffee black. But I do have sugar, if you need it."

"Uh, that's okay. You know what, Gabe, I really should go."

He'd had his eyes on the overly full mugs, but now he looked up at her. "Why?"

"You're sloshing coffee all over." She rescued one of the mugs from him and placed it on the coffee table. "I just realized how late it was."

"Is it because I don't have any milk? I can go borrow some from Mr. Simpson."

"No, it's not that."

"Then what?" He set down the other coffee mug along with the cookies, and then took both of Esperanza's hands in his.

She looked into his eyes. *He's not the enemy,* she told herself. *He's just Gabe.* And in fact his eyes were kind and understanding. "I just . . . I guess I got a little nervous," she admitted.

"About me?"

"About you, about the situation. I'm not very experienced at dating."

"Does it help to know that I'm nervous too?"

"Why are you?" she asked.

He looked around, met her eyes, and then looked away again. "Look, if we're going to have this conversation, let's sit down," he said. "Will you do that? Just for a few minutes?"

He's Gabe, it's safe. "Okay."

"And, look, eat some of these cookies, will you? My mom and sister always give me all this food. They feel sorry for me because I'm a terrible cook, but if I ate everything they gave me I'd look like Santa Claus."

Taking a couple of cookies from the tin, she set them on a napkin in front of her. Then she crossed her legs and crossed her arms over her chest and, thus protected, turned to him expectantly.

He was drinking coffee. He didn't look at her. And suddenly she felt pity for men who always had to make the moves and take the lead position. Suddenly she realized that they could be just as insecure as she felt herself.

"Hey," she said, "Maybe we should just forget about the dating side of things. Maybe we should just turn on the TV and relax."

"Is that what you'd like?" he asked.

"Well, kind of. It seems easier."

He shook his head. "Won't work for me. I'm too attracted to you."

That made her blush.

"I can tell you don't feel that for me yet, at least not as strongly, but do you think it might come?"

Esperanza looked at him. She did think about him a lot, more than she'd ever thought about a man before. "It might," she said cautiously. "But . . . I don't, you know, take all of that lightly."

"Meaning?"

She took a deep breath. "Meaning I won't make love without marriage."

He didn't say anything. And suddenly she realized that it might have sounded like she was pushing for marriage, when in fact that was the last thing on her mind. Well, maybe not the *last*, since Rhonda had brought it up that very evening. But she certainly wasn't longing for it and angling for it.

She hazarded a glance at his face, thinking of how she could explain all of that to him. But he was actually smiling. "What?" she asked defensively. "Do you think I'm old fashioned?"

"No." He moved a little closer and touched her face gently. "I'm glad you feel that way. And I would never push you to do something that went against your beliefs."

"But you said you were attracted—"

"Uh-huh. But that doesn't mean I have to act on it. I have some self-control, Esperanza. I'm not sixteen."

"I know," she said, meeting his eyes, "but you're sort of intense."

He moved fractionally closer. "Is that a bad thing?"

Their eyes were locked. His hand felt warm on her shoulder. And Esperanza couldn't keep her eyes off of his lips, thinking about the gentle kisses they had shared. She swallowed hard to overcome the sudden dryness of her mouth.

"So," he said, leaning closer still, "do you think kissing is wrong?" His lips were just inches away from hers now, but he waited for her answer.

"No, not wrong," she whispered. "Scary, but not wrong."

"Not *just* scary, I hope," he murmured. And then his lips came down over hers.

His kiss was firm enough to tell her he knew what he was doing, but not so aggressive that it upset her. He let her lips go after a moment and put his cheek beside hers, stroking her hair. "Was that scary?" he whispered.

"Not too bad," she whispered back.

He lifted his head to look into her eyes, and there was the age-old certainty of the male in him, the need, the belief that this was necessary and right. She couldn't protest against that certainty.

His large hands cupped her face, then tangled in her hair as he lowered his mouth to hers. She felt his kiss all the way through her body and couldn't restrain a little gasp.

His answer was to deepen the kiss, and Esperanza was transported to another realm entirely, where this closeness, this excitement, this warmth was all that existed. She clung to him, wanting it to go on forever. And when he started to pull away she murmured a protest and brought his face back to hers.

Time stood suspended and there was nothing in the world but love.

When Gabe finally broke away—he even stood and paced over to the darkened window—Esperanza's hand flew to her mouth. She hadn't known herself capable of such feelings.

The word *love* had come into her mind unbidden, and there it stayed as the rest of her slowly came back down to earth.

Was she falling in love with Gabe?

What else could explain this warmth, this sense of being transported? What else could explain this concern, this deep caring that she now felt as she watched him staring out the window into the darkness?

She wanted to be close to him. She wanted to protect him and to be protected. She admired the self-control he had shown, how he hadn't let them get carried away. And perhaps, best of all, was the expanded sense of herself as she considered for the first time the possibility that she, Esperanza Acosta, might be able to have a close relationship and a real family.

But what was *he* thinking now?

When he turned back to face her, she saw confusion and concern on his face. "I'm sorry," he said. "I have some pretty strong feelings where you're concerned."

That made her heart sing, and she risked a smile. "Is that bad?"

"It depends."

"On what?"

"On what your feelings are."

But Esperanza's feelings were such uncharted territory, in a life that had been filled with fear of men, that she didn't know how to explain them. She shook her head helplessly. "I liked kissing you."

He studied her for a moment. Then he came back, sat beside her, and took her hand. "I liked it too," he said. "I liked it a lot. But..."

"If you liked it... what's the bad news?"

He hesitated, looked away, and then looked back at her. "The bad news is, we need to be pretty careful of feelings like that. It would be easy to let them go too far. Unless..." He paused and looked away again.

Again, she felt that concern for him, a sympathy and empathy that made him seem less like a dangerous male adversary and more like an equal, a partner. "Gabe, it's me, Esperanza. Remember? I'm your friend first. I'm not going to judge you for what you say."

He hesitated, and then turned toward her and wrapped both arms loosely around her as she sat forward on the couch. "Okay, here's what I've been thinking. You sure you want to hear this?"

"Yes," she said, meeting his honest eyes, "I'm sure."

"Okay, here goes." He squeezed her a little, then loosened his embrace again. Outside the wind whipped around the building, making a wailing sound. "I'm thinking that we're attracted to each other, *really* attracted. Right? I'm not misreading that?"

Esperanza took a breath, then nodded, suddenly shy again.

"And I'm lonely, but not when I'm with you. You help me feel ... what?" He paused, seeming to search for words. "Better about the past, and hopeful about the future."

"I'm glad," she said.

"And you need a husband to go ahead with your dream of

adoption. Which I've always considered a great way of building families."

"Uh-huh," she whispered. She could hardly breathe.

"And so," he said, leaning away from her so that he could stroke her hair, "it might make sense for us to get married."

9

"Hey, grab that bird! It ran off with my earring!" Mrs. Richardson laughed so hard she almost fell out of her wheelchair.

Esperanza hurried across the Valley View recreation room and, after a brief chase, retrieved the earring from the Amazon parrot that was pecking at it with delight. "Buster! You behave."

"Look at this one, Henry!" One of the other wheelchair-bound residents was chuckling as a bold parakeet climbed up the front of his shirt to perch on his shoulder.

"You should bring those birds back everyday," said Bessie's father.

Bessie came into the room and signaled Esperanza that it was time for the residents' lunch. Reluctantly, Esperanza started caging up the birds she'd brought. Visiting at Valley View was always fun, and engrossing, and the birds had been a big success.

And all the activity and talk had helped her chase away her restless, pounding thoughts about what Gabe had said three nights ago.

Now, as the residents left the lounge, the thoughts came

rushing back. When Gabe had kissed her, she had been so happy that her body could relax, that she could begin to trust a man just a little. The fact that he had backed off, refusing to let their feelings carry them away, helped reassure her even more.

But then he had proposed marriage! Esperanza shook her head, disbelieving, as she wiped away some birdseed that had scattered over a small table. Maybe she had imagined it. Maybe it hadn't really happened.

And then there was the strange way he'd said it: "It might *make sense* for us to get married." It had to be the most unromantic proposal ever made.

She was supposed to be thinking about it. That was the hasty agreement they had made before Gabe took her home. But she couldn't think about it sensibly, even after three days. It was just too bizarre.

"You look preoccupied, my friend," Bessie said as she came into the lounge. "Want to sit a minute? Then I'll help you carry those fellas out."

"Uh, okay." Esperanza didn't exactly want to talk to Bessie about what was going on between her and Gabe. It was all too new in her mind. But unfortunately, Bessie could read her like a picture book.

Bessie flopped down on a couch and put her feet up on the low coffee table in front of it. "So what's going on with you? How's business?"

"Good question," Esperanza said, relieved that Bessie had provided a safe topic. "I have a lot of inquiries from my ads, and the baby birds are coming along great."

"So, that's good, right?"

Esperanza shrugged. "Sure, but it's hard to turn the inquiries into sales. People hear where I'm located and don't want to come to that part of town."

"Can't blame them. It's the only part of Hopewell Corners that has a crime problem."

"Well . . . compared to any big city, the crime rate is low. But you can't argue with people's notions. They associate my neighborhood with car-jackings and robberies, and they stay away."

"How are you going to punt?"

Esperanza smiled at the football metaphor. Bessie loved sports, and had taught Esperanza to be a football fan years ago. "I'm looking at some retail space downtown and at the mall, but it's way out of my price range. So I might consider selling the house and moving to a better part of town, but that's expensive too."

Or I could marry Gabe and move in with him, said a tiny voice in her mind. Immediately she squelched the thought. What a terrible reason to get married—to provide a better location for her business.

Behind them, a woman cleared her throat, and Esperanza half-turned to see Gabe's mother standing in the doorway. "I apologize for interrupting your coffee break," she said with the faintest edge of sarcasm, "but will someone *please* help me find Mrs. Dorothy Halstrom's room?"

"For you I'll interrupt my break, Glenda," Bessie said, standing up with a sigh.

"Oh, Bessie, is that you? I'm so nearsighted."

Esperanza stood too and turned toward the other women. "Hi, Mrs. Montana," she said.

Gabe's mother looked her up and down. "Oh," she said. "It's you."

Esperanza felt herself stiffen. Then she went through a mental dialogue she'd perfected throughout the years. *Even if it's meant personally, it does me no good to take it personally. If she doesn't like me, it's her problem, not mine. I don't have control over what other people think of me. I'm a child of God.* Consciously she relaxed her body and smiled briefly at Mrs. Montana. "Uh-huh, it's me," she said. Then she walked over to the bird cages and started bagging her supplies.

Behind her, she heard Bessie direct Mrs. Montana to a room down the hall. She allowed herself a mischievous thought. What would Mrs. Montana think if she knew her precious son Gabe had proposed to her the night before?

She was carrying her first load down the stairs when Bessie caught up with her, a birdcage in each hand. "So what's wrong between you and Glenda Montana?" she asked.

"She thinks I'm after her son," Esperanza explained as they walked along the main hall.

Bessie waited until they'd passed a couple of residents, and then asked, "Are you?"

"You know me better than that."

They hurried the birds into Esperanza's car and she started the engine, turning up the heater full blast. To her surprise, Bessie climbed in the passenger side. "Tell me what's going on," she said.

Esperanza looked at Bessie. Even though she usually kept her problems to herself, she was bursting to tell someone that Gabe Montana, the man so admired in Hopewell Corners, had proposed to *her*.

"Well," she said, "don't repeat this, okay, but Gabe asked me to marry him."

"No!" Bessie's eyes widened. "What did you say?"

"I'm supposed to be thinking about it. But it's a crazy idea. He doesn't know me all that well."

"You've only dated him a few times, right?"

Esperanza nodded. "He's crazy. I don't know what he's thinking, except that I need a husband to adopt babies, and he wants to get married again because he misses Melissa." She stared through the windshield at the dreary winter landscape.

"He put it more like a business proposition than a marriage proposal."

"Ouch. How do you feel about Gabe, anyway?"

"He's a good man. I admire him."

"And . . . is there any spark between you?"

Esperanza blushed and looked down at her hands in her lap. Slowly, she nodded.

"Well, then," Bessie said briskly, "this is good news, right? He might be the one."

"We hardly know each other!"

"Then get to know each other."

"I don't know—"

"Look, honey," Bessie said, turning so that she faced Esperanza, "I know you. I'll just bet you're thinking about running the other way. But give him a chance, all right? He *is* a good man. And the fact that he's jumping in so fast must mean he has strong feelings for you."

"Or that he's desperate to replace Melissa."

"She died three years ago. That doesn't sound like desperation to me."

"I don't know."

"Think about it. Get to know him better. Don't just say no automatically." Bessie glanced at her watch. "I've got to get back to work. We just used up my lunch hour. But I got something better than lunch: good news about you."

"Thanks for talking," Esperanza said as Bessie climbed out of the car. "I'll call you soon."

LATER THAT WEEK, after she'd spent the afternoon at home hand-feeding all the baby birds and cleaning cages, Esperanza sighed over the ledger sheets in front of her. She just couldn't see a way to move to a better location, not without going further out on a financial limb than she dared to go. And yet she had lost another sale earlier that afternoon when a potential customer had flat-out refused to come to her neighborhood.

Closing her eyes, she bent her head and stilled her swirling thoughts. Once her mind was clear, she prayed: *Lord, I can't find the way out of this, but You're all powerful. Grant me Your wisdom.*

After a few minutes of silence, she felt her spirits lift. She doodled aimlessly on her desk blotter, and then looked at what she'd drawn. A truck. Why a truck? She never drew trucks.

And then she thought of it: she could *deliver* the baby birds to people's houses.

But people wanted to choose their own bird out of a number. Plus, the babies were so sensitive to the cold.

Immediately her problem solving skills kicked in. A van, then. A van outfitted with three or four cages, so that people could choose. And carefully heated to keep the birds safe.

Thank you, Lord. She'd certainly need to refine the idea, but it was a good possibility.

She walked over to Paco's cage. The big red macaw looked better; with a healthy diet and as much attention as he could tolerate—which wasn't much—his feathers had started growing back and he had stopped pulling them out.

"You're so pretty," she crooned in a soft voice. "Come on over here. Let me scratch your head."

"I'm a pretty bird."

Esperanza stared. It was the first time she had heard Paco say words, though she'd heard him screeching many times. His voice was gutteral but perfectly understandable. How many other phrases did the bird know?

She tried to get him to repeat the phrase, but in true parrot fashion, he refused to perform on command. "Independent, are you? I get that."

Paco didn't respond, but he scooted slowly toward the side of the cage where she stood, and bent his large red head. Cautiously she lifted her hand. It was the parrot's way of inviting her to pet him, but she still had the scar from his bite weeks before.

If she didn't try touching him, though, he would never get tame. Gently she reached out a finger and scratched the bird's head.

Paco responded by turning his head from side to side, making sure she reached every spot. "Yeah, that feels good, doesn't it," she murmured, keeping her voice calm and soothing.

The bird lifted his head and touched her hand with his beak. Esperanza remained perfectly still. She knew that parrots used their beaks to test a perch or explore a new object. But a macaw of Paco's size could also break a person's finger.

Paco opened his beak and put it around her finger.

"You're a pretty bird," she said, focusing all of her attention on the bird, willing him to be gentle.

At her words, the large bird lifted his head and cocked it, looking at her with one eye. Then he scooted away on his perch and began preening himself.

Esperanza let out the breath she'd been holding. "Good boy, Paco," she praised him. "Good boy."

As she turned away Paco repeated, "I'm a pretty bird."

"You *are* pretty," she tossed back over her shoulder, smiling.

And then she saw Gabe standing in the doorway.

Esperanza started back. "How'd you get in? You scared me."

"Sorry," he said. "I didn't want to disturb you while you were working with Paco. Rhonda let me in."

"Oh. I didn't know she was home." Walking slowly toward him, she felt the inrush of all kinds of emotions—awkwardness, excitement, fear—and, overwhelmed, she stopped a good ten feet away from him.

"You're doing a great job with Paco," he said. "It took some courage to let that beak near your hand, after what happened last time."

"I was scared. But if he's ever going to get tame, I have to risk a few bites."

He nodded, leaning against the doorway, looking at her. Around them, the birds chattered, but the moment still felt private. And there was a question in his eyes, one she'd been avoiding, one she knew she would have to answer sooner or later.

As it turned out, it was sooner. "Have you thought about what we talked about the other day?" he asked.

"I've thought about it some."

"Did you make a decision?"

She hesitated. "Let's . . . sit down a minute."

"*That* doesn't sound good." He followed her to the small group of chairs that she kept by her desk for her customers.

Esperanza's heart was pounding to the point where it was hard for her to talk, or think. But she'd avoided him long enough. "Look," she blurted out finally, "I think we can try to know each other better. We can go out. But we aren't ready to make a decision."

He sat still, looking at her, for such a long time that Esperanza finally looked away. Then he leaned forward and touched her hand, shaking his head slowly. "That's not enough."

"What do you mean, it's not enough? What's not enough?"

"Casual dating. Esperanza, we've worked together—"

"For two months," she interrupted.

"I've worked with you, taken care of kids with you, talked with you," he continued as if she hadn't spoken. "You've met my family. You and I share a lot of the same interests and habits."

"But you don't know me well enough!"

"I know everything I need to know. I want to marry you." His eyes burned with sincerity, with certainty. There was even a trace of a smile on his face.

She seized on that. "Why are you smiling? Do you feel so sure of me, that I'll say yes?"

"Not at all," he said. "I'm incredibly nervous. It's just that I've spent a lot of time thinking it over this past week, and I really do feel certain. But beyond this point, I don't have control. You have to make the decision."

"Look, you know some about my background, but not everything. It's hard for me to trust you. That's just the way I am."

"Do you care for me?"

"Well... yes. A lot."

"Do you respect me?"

"You know I do." It was nothing but the truth. She had seen his skilled, compassionate leadership of the adoption agency, and she had seen him deal with an important stage of his grief about his wife and child in an emotionally-open way.

He wrapped his hand around hers. "Are you attracted to me physically?"

Her cheeks flamed as she half-smiled at him. "Oh, just a little."

"Okay," he said, "then listen. I've been studying the adoption guidelines and the decisions the caseworkers have been making. Normally they won't let a couple adopt until they've been married at least a year."

"Makes sense."

"So the sooner we make a decision, the sooner we can get started. I think we might even be able to hurry things along a little bit."

She stared at him. "You want to adopt? Rather than having your own kids?"

"I wouldn't mind having children of my own," he said. "But I'm involved with the agency because I felt called to it. I believe in adoption. And I'm starting to see how it all fits together. I'd like us to adopt at least one baby, maybe more. Maybe a lot more."

"Where would we put them?" she asked to stall him from the main question. She couldn't help but let in the vision that was forming in her mind. She could have her dream, her lifelong dream. With Gabe's status, connections, and financial stability, she was sure that they would be chosen as adoptive parents. And it could happen sooner rather than later. No more waiting. No more fighting the system. No more disappointments.

But Gabe was saying something else. "My grandmother passed on last year, and left her house to us kids. I made the decision to buy the others out, and they agreed to it. It needed some work, which is why I'm still living in the apartment now, but as soon as we get married, we can move in."

He sounded like it was a done deal. But his voice was still tight, and he was talking more and faster than she'd heard him talk before, and she realized that he had spoken the truth about being nervous.

"There's room for your birds," he said. "There's a huge heated sun porch that would be perfect. So you could keep up the business."

"Where's the house?" she asked, still stalling over the main question.

"On a big wooded lot right outside of Hopewell Corners," he said. "It's perfect for kids." He hesitated, then added, "We can make your dreams come true, Esperanza."

She looked at him and then looked away, biting her lip. Thoughts and images raced in her mind. Adopting babies who needed homes. Raising them in a beautiful house, with a mother *and* a father. Having a real family ... at last.

Her heart pounded, and she didn't know if it was excitement or fear. The pace of Gabe's courtship and decision-making left her breathless. But wasn't the picture he'd painted everything she had ever dreamed of? Wasn't it the *only* way she could fulfill her dream?

And yet . . . there was a question she had to ask. And it was the hardest one of all, because the potential for hurt and rejection was so great. She cleared her throat. "So . . . Gabe. How do you feel about me? Do you, well, you know, *love* me?" The last words came out as a husky whisper.

He looked at the floor for a moment, and then met her eyes. His hands were still gripping hers. "I've come to care very deeply for you," he said. "I think love is an action word, and I pledge to you right now that I'll love you faithfully and the best way I know how."

It wasn't exactly what she wanted to hear, and yet she believed everything he said. Maybe it was enough.

"I'm not going to ask you the same question," he continued, "because I believe that love grows with time. I know married love goes way beyond that romantic, Valentine's Day feeling everyone seems to be looking for."

The peal of the doorbell startled both of them. Esperanza heard Rhonda opening the door. Then she called, "Eppie! Come here a minute."

"I'll be right back," she said to Gabe.

When she got out to the front hallway, Rhonda grabbed her arm. "Are you crazy?" she asked. "Say yes before he changes his mind!"

"Who's at the door?" Esperanza asked, bewildered.

"No one's at the door, you fool. I just wanted to get you out here to tell you, stop messing around and marry the guy."

"You were listening?"

"Of course I was listening! Honey, think back. When did either of us ever get a chance like this? Grab it! Go for it!"

"Ssssh!"

Rhonda lowered her voice. "I know you. I know how scared you get, and I know why. But I'm telling you, this is your main chance. For Pete's sake, I'd marry him if he asked me. He's a great guy, he's fun, he's got a steady job, a house in the country, and he wants to adopt babies. If you'd filled out a request form for exactly what you wanted in life, this would be it. Don't blow it because you're scared. Do it!"

"I . . . you really think so?" She met Rhonda's eyes. Rhonda knew her better than almost anyone. Rhonda knew all her secrets and shared a similar unhappy past. If Rhonda thought it was a good thing, that tipped the scales.

Her foster sister was smiling. "I really think so," she said. "Now get in there and give him a big kiss, and say yes!" She hugged Esperanza quickly, then turned her around and gave her a little shove toward the back of the house. "Go on!"

"I think . . . I might just do that. Thanks, Rhonda."

Right before she reached the bird room, she paused and closed her eyes. Rhonda was right. She had prayed for a way to fulfill her dream, every day for years. This wasn't the way she had imagined it would happen; she had thought she would adopt and raise children alone. But wasn't this a better plan?

Guide me, Father. She let the prayer permeate her for a moment, took a deep breath and walked through the doorway.

"Who was at the door?" Gabe asked as she walked back toward the chair where he still sat, leaning forward, elbows on knees, his hands clasped tightly.

"Oh, just . . . a good angel," she said lightly. Instead of sitting, she knelt in front of him and took his clenched hands in her own much smaller ones. "Gabe, thank you for offering me so much. It's more than I ever dreamed of having."

He cocked his head to one side, studying her. "Does that mean yes or no?"

She took another deep breath, her heart expanding inside her, still feeling that loving warmth surrounding her, protecting her, cherishing her. "It means yes," she said softly.

10

"There's still time to change your mind." Gabe's mother's voice was higher-pitched than usual.

Gabe looked up from his brother's tie, which he was tightening because John was so impossibly uncomfortable in a suit that he couldn't do it himself. "Mom, the wedding starts in five minutes. And I'm not backing out."

The previous two months had rushed by quickly, with Christmas celebrations bumping up against preparing for a wedding. But Gabe had felt no impulse to change his mind. Instead, he was more and more eager to begin married life with Esperanza.

His mother adjusted her already perfect corsage. Despite her objections to the marriage, she would never dream of looking less-than-appropriate as the mother of the groom. "I just can't imagine what people will think when that trashy stepsister, or foster-sister, or whatever she is, struts down the aisle in that dress. Did you see it, Gabriel? Did you?"

"I saw it," Gabe said, sighing.

"I kinda liked the dress," John said with an exaggerated leer. "And you gotta admit, Rhonda wears it well."

"Half a size smaller and she'd *burst* out of it," their mother said. "They're calling me in, dear. Are you sure you want to do this?"

"I'm sure. Now get out there. Bessie's going to beat you to the unity candle."

"Common. I always thought Bessie Ingram was just common." But she raised her chin and pulled back her shoulders, in classic charm school style, before marching out to join Bessie in lighting the candle that supposedly symbolized two families becoming one.

Moments later, it was Gabe's turn, and he gladly let his brother and his best friend steer him to the altar. His own nerves were on edge.

As he watched Tanisha come down the aisle first, head high, with only an occasional nervous glance down at the basket of flowers she carried, he thought about the dreams he had for life with Esperanza. It could work, it really could, but it depended on her being able to open herself to him. He had seen glimpses of that openness, and he offered up a hasty, fervent prayer that it would continue, that Esperanza would gradually trust him enough to relax completely.

Now his sister Bianca came down the aisle, looking beautiful. She was followed by Rhonda. From behind him, where his family occupied the front pews, Gabe heard his mother click her tongue in disapproval.

The bridesmaids' dresses were a deeper shade of pink than Tanisha's had been. And Rhonda had basically the same dress as his sister wore. But while Bianca's dress looked perfectly modest, Rhonda's was cut low enough to reveal her substantial cleavage. The rest of the dress was tight, too. And as she came into full view, half-an-aisle behind his sister, he saw the same slightly protruding stomach that marked most of the young women who came to the agency to make adoption plans.

Whoa. That was news to him. He glanced around the church and saw that every eye in the place was glued to Rhonda, male and female alike. He doubted that most of the men were focusing on her stomach, but some of the women, more attuned to the look of early pregnancy, had surely noticed the same thing he had.

A niggling misgiving twisted his gut. He had known Esperanza didn't have an ordinary family, of course, but he had come to terms with that fact, had decided that he wasn't going to look for another all-American Melissa, but to follow his heart where it led him. But he couldn't help but wonder if he and Esperanza would end up caring for Rhonda and her illegitimate baby. He wondered why Esperanza hadn't told him about Rhonda's condition. Most of all, he shook his head at the defiant attitude that made Rhonda flaunt both her pregnancy and her abundant, fertile sexiness at her foster-sister's wedding.

And then he saw Esperanza standing in the rear doorway of the church, escorted by Bessie's father, and he forgot all about Rhonda. Because Esperanza looked gorgeous. She rarely wore dresses, and here she was in a dress to end all dresses. Like her, it was simple and unornamented, but the fitted bodice emphasized her fragile slimness. The simple veil, white against her dark hair, gave her an exotic beauty that caused more than one intake of breath in Gabe's hearing.

He couldn't believe he was fortunate enough to have her as his wife.

To bed her tonight—maybe.

As she started down the aisle, Gabe felt a restless desire to touch that soft skin, to run his hands through her long, silky hair. The memory of the sweet kisses they had shared left him hungry to taste her more deeply.

But he wasn't going to push her. She was shy, and inhibited, and he suspected that the harassment she had undergone as a foster child had left some serious scars. The last thing he wanted was to join the cluster of groping, ravenous men that haunted her psyche.

No, he would be gentle. Gentle and patient. And if tonight wasn't to be the night, he was prepared to deal with it.

But he couldn't help hoping he could seduce her shyness away.

When she reached the front of the church, Bessie's father reached up from his wheelchair to give her a hug and then turned to Gabe. "You treat her right, hear?" he rasped in a voice audible to at least half the church. "She's a gem."

"I know," he said, grasping the older man's hand. "I'll take good care of her."

Mr. Ingram nodded and pivoted his mechanized wheelchair, heading to the side aisle of the church, and Gabe turned to Esperanza. He saw the top of her head, ringed her veil's pearly band. Why was she looking down?

And then the minister urged them forward and joined their hands, and she had to look up.

Her eyes were sick with fear.

Instantly, his baser thoughts vanished. He wanted to take her in his arms and soothe her worries away. He wished he had spent more time talking and reassuring her before the wedding, but the preparations had been so quick and hectic that they hadn't had much time together. During the past week, they had barely seen each other.

Now, listening to the minister's soothing voice without hearing it, Gabe tried to fix Esperanza's gaze, to reassure her with his eyes. But she kept looking away, licking her lips. Her hands were sweating. He was afraid she was going to bolt like a frightened animal.

It kept getting worse during the ceremony. When they moved up to the altar with the best man and maid of honor,

Gabe saw Rhonda practically pushing Esperanza into place. When he took her hand to place the ring on it, he felt the trembling. And when they took their vows, Esperanza hesitated a long time.

Gabe couldn't believe it. Was she going to back out in front of all these people? Was she really that afraid of him, of commitment, of marriage? Was all of this a huge mistake?

"You may answer, 'I do'," the minister repeated quietly.

He saw her draw in her breath.

"Hurry up, Miss Esperanza!" Tanisha said in a stage whisper. "We be fallin' asleep pretty soon!"

A smile creased Esperanza's face, the first Gabe had seen on her today. She straightened up. "I do," she said with only a slight huskiness in her voice.

Gabe let out the breath he'd been holding. And in that moment, as the minister said a few more words and offered a prayer, he realized anew how much he wanted this marriage and wanted it to work.

No, he didn't feel the same way about Esperanza that he had about Melissa. But he believed in what they were doing, believed it was for the good of both of them. He had lived alone too long. Their love would grow and they would build a strong family.

When he kissed her in front of the church, he felt her pull back ever so slightly. "It'll be okay," he whispered, squeezing her shoulders.

She smiled a little—and backed up a little more.

~

ESPERANZA WAS glad they had agreed to keep the wedding small and the reception simple. She couldn't have survived the hours of drinking and dancing that characterized most weddings, especially the Catholic ones Gabe's family was used to.

A simple cake-and-punch gathering in the church basement was bad enough, given the animosity of certain parts of Gabe's family, and given the fear that had her stomach twisted in tight knots.

She had come so close to backing out.

The past few weeks had been hectic, and she had gone through them with a slight, pleasant numbness, doing what Rhonda, Bessie, and Gabe's sister Bianca told her to do. She'd spent time with Gabe, but they had kept it light.

No heavy discussions.

No intense, passionate kisses.

As a result, she had felt far less anxiety than she would have expected; she had slept like a lamb each night. And when she thought about the marriage, she figured that her relaxed feelings were proof that she was doing the right thing.

The numbness had started to break up, though, as they had arrived at the church. As she put on her wedding dress, she felt a sense of dread coming on. And when handed her flowers, she hadn't wanted to take them.

Rhonda had seen what was happening first. "Don't be a fool," she had hissed at the back of the church as they were waiting for the processional. "This is what you've always wanted. He's a great guy. You're going to be so happy together. It's a dream come true."

"He's a good man," Bessie's father had added. "I've known him for years. He's rock-solid. I'd trust him with my own daughter any day of the week."

That had bolstered her enough to get her down the aisle. But as she had approached Gabe, breathtakingly handsome in his black tux, she had seen something in his eyes that had brought the fears rushing back.

It was something... primitive. Predatory. Possessive.

And though it had faded into the background as he'd looked at her, as he had seen her obvious terror, it was there, and she knew it was there.

It was what she had always run from. It was the reason she had never wanted to marry.

And she was kicking herself for that pleasant daze in which she'd spent the past few weeks.

Only Tanisha's voice had allowed her to go through with the final vows. Hearing Tanisha had reminded her that, though Gabe, she could achieve the only dream she'd ever had, and help some desperate babies and children in the process.

It was the time in between marrying him and having the shield of a large adopted family that worried her.

"Look out," Rhonda whispered through a mouthful of cake. "The wicked witch is looking at us."

Esperanza looked up from her wedding cake to meet Gabe's mother's eyes across the crowded room. The older woman fumbled with her handbag, pulled out some sort of pillbox, and tossed back pills with a large gulp of punch.

"I guess the wedding gave her some headache," Esperanza murmured to Rhonda. "Uh-oh. Here she comes."

As Gabe's mother walked toward them, a purposeful look on her face, Rhonda stepped up beside Esperanza, even a little in front of her. It was a relief. Rhonda had scarcely left her side during the reception, even though there were a few good-looking men trying to catch her eye. Rhonda had her faults, but she was standing by Esperanza like a sister, and for someone who had no blood relatives at all, that was a gift beyond pearls.

"So," Gabe's mother said without preamble when she reached them, "it looks like *you're* the one who should have been getting married." She was looking at Rhonda.

Esperanza gasped at the rudeness of her remark. "What's

that supposed to mean?" she asked, putting her arm around Rhonda.

"She's showing," Mrs. Montana said, gesturing at Rhonda's midsection.

Esperanza looked, saw the small bulge, and felt her mouth drop open. "Why didn't you tell me?" she asked when she could form the words.

"As if you didn't know about it," Mrs. Montana said. "I see what you're up to. You're hoping my son will support both of you. I suppose we can expect you to start showing any day now too," she added to Esperanza.

"What?" Esperanza looked at her blankly, still trying to process Rhonda's news.

"It's obvious to me now. I don't know why I didn't think of it before. The hurry-up wedding, the quiet ceremony . . . it's all falling into place."

Esperanza was speechless.

"Look," Rhonda hissed, "I'd deck you for that, except I don't want to ruin my sister's wedding reception. She's not that type. She and Gabe haven't even—"

Gabe seemed to appear out of nowhere. "What haven't we done?" he asked..

"Your mother," Esperanza said, forcing herself to keep her voice low and even, "thinks we got married because I'm pregnant. You might want to talk to her about that." And then she grabbed Rhonda's hand and pulled her toward a row of folding chairs at the far side of the fellowship hall.

"Sit down," she ordered, shoving Rhonda toward a chair. And then she flopped down herself with total disregard for her dress bunching up beneath her.

Rhonda was staring back toward Mrs. Montana with murder in her eyes. "What a witch on wheels. I feel sorry for you, Eppie.

You got a great guy, but the mother-in-law is almost bad enough to cancel him out."

"Forget about her," Esperanza said impatiently. "Are you really pregnant? Why didn't you tell me? Why didn't I notice?" she added, feeling guilty.

Rhonda leaned back and looked up at the ceiling. She let her hands rest on the tiny mound of her stomach with the ancient protective gesture of a mother-to-be, erasing Esperanza's last doubt. "I didn't want to spoil your wedding plans," she said. "I knew you'd worry. I've been wearing sweats and baggy dresses to cover it up. But I guess I messed up your wedding anyway." She glanced down at her dress. "When I tried this thing on, it wasn't this tight. Wonder if everyone noticed."

"Oh, I doubt it," Esperanza said, though now that she looked at Rhonda closely she couldn't believe she'd missed it. "Anyway, the men were probably looking at your chest, not your stomach."

"Yeah, well, that got a little bigger too, in the past couple of months."

Esperanza shook her head. "I can't believe you didn't tell me. How long have you known?"

"I knew for sure a month ago. Before that, I didn't want to believe it."

"You and Danny are . . . what?"

"Well, we're not getting married, if that's what you're asking. In fact, we're close to breaking up."

"That's what I thought. I know you haven't been seeing him too often."

Rhonda sighed. "I quit drinking because of the baby, and going out to bars isn't much fun when you don't drink. So I guess I'm not as much fun anymore either. And he's not ready to be tied down, that's pretty clear."

"What are we going to do?"

"It's my problem, Eppie, not yours."

"Don't be silly. Of course it's my problem too."

But Rhonda shook her head with a firmness and finality Esperanza had never seen in her before. "No, uh-uh. I made my own trouble, and now I'm getting out of it my own way."

"You don't mean—"

Rhonda's eyes widened. "Of course not! Although," she said reluctantly, "Danny did ask if I'd consider getting rid of the baby. Which is another reason we're about on the rocks."

"Oh, honey. I'm sorry." Esperanza put her arms around Rhonda and hugged her tightly. "You know I'm there for you," she whispered into Rhonda's teased and hairsprayed hair. "I'll help you take care of the baby."

"We'll see," Rhonda said, pulling away. She brushed her fingers under her eyes. "Is my mascara messed up?"

Esperanza thumbed a tiny smear from Rhonda's cheek. "There. Perfect."

"Good. Because everyone's looking at us, even though they're pretending not to. You're the bride, you'd better get back over there. And I saw this one really cute guy I want to meet before this party breaks up."

Esperanza shook her head, smiling a little, as Rhonda led her back toward the small crowd. Rhonda was irrepressible, and she would be all right. And Esperanza would do whatever she could to help.

As they wound up the four-hour drive to the rustic cabin where they'd agreed to spend their honeymoon, Gabe's hands sweated on the steering wheel. When he glanced over at Esperanza and saw her tightly-clenched jaw, he knew that she was nervous too.

"It looks like good skiing," he said to cut through the loaded silence.

"Does it? I wouldn't know." She snuck a sideways glance at him. "You're sure you don't mind teaching me how?"

"No. Cross-country skiing is easy. You'll like it." In fact, Gabe wished they had arranged to get here in daylight, so that they could do something like that together. Something physical, something relaxing. Something to bring them closer before bedtime.

But despite the afternoon wedding and the short reception, it was nearly ten o'clock by the time they reached the end of the long dirt road and saw the cabin, covered in snow. Gabe glanced over at Esperanza, wondering suddenly if she would have preferred a big-city or Caribbean honeymoon. This cabin had been in their family for years, and it was definitely nice inside, but it wasn't exactly Paris.

She was looking at it with one of the few smiles he had seen from her all day. "Gabe, it's wonderful. It's just the type of place I love. Does it have a fireplace?"

"Fireplace, fully-equipped kitchen, loft, hot tub . . . the works," he said, relieved that she seemed content. "It's supposed to be all ready, but let's check to make sure."

Snow had drifted over the previously-cleared sidewalk, giving Gabe an excuse to take Esperanza's hand. Once she was safely inside, he didn't let go. Couldn't, really. The sight of her breathlessly-rosy face, her long eyelashes kissed by snowflakes, started a heavy, aching need in him. Holding on to her was the only thing that helped.

"It's so nice!" she said, looking around in obvious delight. "I thought you said it was rustic. This looks elegant!"

He led her around, showing her everything. She admired the kitchen and exclaimed over the deck with its hot tub. Gabe lifted the cover and dipped their linked hands into the water, smiling to find that it was warm. Exactly according to his instructions.

A fire had been prepared in the fireplace, needing only a

match to get it started, so he dropped her hand and lit it. As they stood, watching the blaze ignite all the tiny twigs and flame into life, he put his arm around her shoulders. And he felt her stiffen. He shut his eyes for a moment, wondering if the day was going to end the way he had hoped.

Something in him, some primitive part he barely knew, wouldn't let him back off. He moved behind her and massaged her sweater-clad shoulders, gently and then with increasing pressure. "Are you tense?" he asked. Dumb question, feeling the knotted muscles of her shoulders and neck, but he felt like they needed to talk.

"A little. Gabe . . ." She twisted away from him and crossed her arms over her chest in a classic move of self-protection. "Don't we need to get the suitcases out of the truck?"

He let his hands drop to his sides. "I guess. Yeah, sure. You stay here, I can get them."

As he made two trips, bringing in their suitcases, ski equipment, and some last-minute food his sister had insisted on including, he tried to calm down by talking to himself. *Take it easy. You've got plenty of time. It doesn't have to happen tonight.* He even stood outside for a few minutes with his coat open, literally cooling off.

But when he went back inside and saw her sitting on the thick rug in front of the fire, his instincts came thoroughly alive.

She was his woman now. And he wanted, *needed* to cement that alliance in the ancient way of male and female.

He leaned the skis against the wall in the entryway, carried the suitcases up to the loft, washed his face and brushed his teeth, and then came downstairs. She still sat in front of the fire as if mesmerized by the flickering flames.

Slowly he approached her. He sank down behind her, inches away but not touching. She glanced back over her shoulder at him. "Everything inside?" she asked in a bright tone that betrayed her nervousness.

"It's all taken care of," he said, wrapping his arms around her. "We can relax."

But she resisted his embrace, shrugged and wiggled out of his arms, and turned to face him. "Look," she said, "we've got to get a few things straight."

11

Esperanza picked at the fur rug, the skin of some unfortunate animal, but boy was it soft. Gabe had told her they could wait about the wedding night, the consummation of their marriage. But since they'd arrived at the cabin, he had been acting so physical.

Like now. He was still sitting close to her, and his fingers couldn't seem to stop themselves from playing with her hair. He was big, and yes, incredibly good-looking in casual jeans and a flannel shirt. The collar opened to show dark chest hair, and his broad shoulders strained his flannel shirt. She'd never seen him dressed this casually, she realized. And, she'd never been this alone with him. There had always been Rhonda, or his family, or Tanisha, or their co-workers nearby or arriving soon. Or a reason to go home soon.

Now, they had an entire week to themselves.

And she was a wreck about it. But she had better get it all out into the open, so she knew what she was dealing with. "I need to know," she said slowly, "what you expect from me this week."

"What I expect," he said, staring into the fire. "Hmmm. I

certainly expect my dinners prepared at exactly six each night. A hot breakfast at seven a.m., served to me in bed. My slippers..."

She slapped him lightly on the arm. "Dream on!" But he had made her laugh, had loosened, at least slightly, the net of tension that had been tightening around her all day. "I mean it, Gabe. I want to know about, you know . . ." She trailed off, not sure how to say it.

"Bed?" he asked bluntly.

She nodded, studying the white fur of the rug.

"Well . . . we did talk about it before. I told you I can wait until you're ready."

"But will it be hard for you?"

A short laugh escaped him. "Yes."

Esperanza felt herself blushing. She didn't know what to say.

"Hey," he said, touching her chin, making her meet his eyes. "What are you worried about? That I'll force you?"

"No, no, not that. But . . . I don't want you to be unhappy. Like you've gotten a bad deal or something. I know how important sex is to a man, and if you can't do without it then . . . we can go ahead. I mean, I promised you we would do it eventually, that it wouldn't be a marriage in name only."

"I'd like it to be a little more mutual than that, Esperanza. I don't want you suffering through lovemaking because you think I've got some itch that has to be scratched."

She wrapped her arms around her knees. Although she was staring into the fire, she felt frozen.

He put an arm around her, and she couldn't help it, she stiffened. Rather than backing off, he used his other hand to brush back her hair. "Look, Esperanza, I'm going to be honest. I really do hope we can consummate the marriage, if not tonight, then this week. It would mean a lot to me. But it would only mean a lot if you came to me willingly."

She turned her head to the side and rested it on her arms, looking at him. His voice was kind and steady.

"I'd like to try," he said. "Maybe we'll just kiss, I don't know. But . . ." He tipped his head to one side so that he was looking into her eyes, " . . . would you let me hold you, and touch you, knowing that it can stop whenever you say the word?"

She breathed in his scent, mixed with wood smoke. Could she trust him, once he started? But she had to, at some point. She had to make that leap of faith. And anyway, how bad could it be? She would survive it, anyway. "All right," she said.

A smile creased his face and he slowly shook his head, his eyes never leaving hers. "You sound like you've agreed to be drawn and quartered," he said. And then, to her surprise, he rose gracefully to his feet and left the room.

A moment later he was back with a bottle of wine, a corkscrew, and two glasses. He set it down, then turned on a classical music station and found big pillows to stack behind them.

"You're setting up a real romantic scene," she forced herself to say, jokingly.

"If I can't try to seduce my wife, who can I seduce?" he asked. And then he sat down, opened the wine and poured them each a glass, and settled next to her with the pillows propping them up, his arm around her, facing the fire. "So," he said, "tell me about Rhonda. What's going on?"

Gabe had hit on probably the only topic that could have distracted her from her nervousness. Leaning back into the comfortable, warm bulk of his shoulder, she told him what she'd learned, and how Rhonda seemed to be coping with her pregnancy. From there they went on to talk about the people at the wedding, who they'd each seen and talked to, what they'd heard.

When he refilled her wine glass she laughed. "I hardly ever

drink, you know," she said. "Are you trying to take advantage of that?"

"Will it work?" He set down the bottle.

She shrugged. "I feel more relaxed."

"Good." His arm was around her again. He leaned over and kissed her, the lightest of kisses, barely brushing her mouth.

"Mmmm."

"You like that?"

"Uh-huh."

His lips pressed hers again, more firmly. His tongue flicked and teased, and she opened herself to him without thinking about it. And then she was lost, for with skillful restraint, as if there were all the time in the world, he lazily, rhythmically took her to another place, another plane.

She hardly knew how it happened, but she was on her back on the rug and he was leaning over her. One large hand stroked her hair, her arm, her stomach while he looked at her with warm, loving eyes. "Feel good?" he asked.

"Uh-huh." She was drifting pleasantly, her eyes closing.

His hand moved to the buttons of her flannel shirt. He undid the top one, then the second, and her eyes flew open. "I thought you might be getting too warm," he murmured, a lazy smile in his voice.

Her heart was pounding, but she held onto the relaxed feeling his caresses had built. "Thoughtful of you," she said.

He undid another button, and then his hand stilled. "No bra?"

"I don't ... really need one," she said, worrying suddenly that her body wouldn't appeal to him if they ever did get around to making love.

"I'm with you there," he said, kissing her lightly again. As he did, his hand spread the edges of her shirt and crept inside.

She drew in her breath and her heartbeat quickened.

The surges of pleasure caught her by surprise. The flashes of fear didn't. They were just her normal responses to anyone touching her.

But no one had done *this* before. No one had touched her body with attention to what she wanted, what she responded to. Gabe watched and listened, and his light caresses responded to her every intake of breath.

She wanted to tell him, to thank him. "It feels good," she finally managed, surprised at the huskiness of her own voice.

Tentatively at first, she touched him. She traced the rigid muscles of his chest, the bulges that showed his arms' strength. She touched that shiny, slightly wavy hair and ran her fingers over his neck, under his collar. And she tasted the entirely new flavor of enjoying his responses to her touch—his closed eyes, his sharply drawn-in breath, and, once, a low groan.

When his hands moved farther, though, she tensed. She was torn between wanting to please him, wanting this to go on, and the memories that clenched her stomach and made her want to curl up into a little ball. Gabe didn't realize how it was for her. He couldn't. He was understanding, but he didn't understand. How incredibly awful that the things he was doing with respect and affection were the same things bad men did to women with disrespect and force.

But he was being kinder than any man had ever been, and she wanted him to feel pleasure too. She let her hand splay against his chest, inside his shirt.

His audible intake of breath told her how much their slow, relaxed pleasuring had cost him. She jerked her hand away, her heart pounding.

Now was when she expected him to get overly aggressive. She knew from experience that men lost control once they got aroused. Wary, she tried to ease herself out from under his arm, to slide a few inches away from him.

His head propped up on one elbow, he watched her. He made no protest when she slid away from him. He even smiled a little, looking interested and concerned.

When she saw that he wasn't going to push it, she stopped moving. Now she was propped on her side too.

His glance strayed to her chest, and a muscle in his cheek jumped. She realized what he was looking at and pulled the edges of her shirt together. Wanting to cover her scars as much as her chest.

"Had enough for tonight?" he asked in a voice that was only slightly strained.

She stared at him, surprised. "Have you?"

He actually laughed as he ran his hands through his hair and buttoned his shirt—had she unbuttoned it?

He knelt by the fireplace and adjusted the screen. Then he rose to his feet and held out a hand to pull her up.

She stood, confused by his change of mood. "What are you doing?"

He reached toward her chest and she stiffened, but he only buttoned her buttons as if she were a child. "I think we should go out for a walk."

"I thought you wanted to—"

"Not tonight," he said.

"But you said it would mean a lot to you."

"I know." He was already over by the hooks at the cabin door, shrugging into his coat, locating hers and holding it for her."

Slowly she walked over and put the coat on. "Gabe, I . . . Are you sure?"

"Uh-huh." He handed her some mittens and a hat, put on his own gloves, and opened the cabin door. "Look, the moon's out. Come on."

The cold night air shocked her fire-warmed skin, and she didn't know if she felt more relieved or more disappointed. She knew he had to be frustrated. From all of her experiences, a man who didn't get what he wanted in the sexual department was at least out of sorts, and usually mean.

But Gabe had his arm around her shoulders and was pointing out constellations as if he didn't have a care in the world. The knot of apprehension that had tightened in her chest all day finally loosened.

He wasn't going to force her or even push her. He had control of himself. It was a relief. And now that her fear was gone, she noticed in herself just the slightest curiosity about what might have happened next, what that next step might feel like.

∽

THREE NIGHTS LATER, Gabe watched Esperanza brushing her hair before bed and wondered, moodily, if he could make it through the rest of the week.

That first night in front of the fire, he had made a decision that he wasn't going to push lovemaking on her. It was all too apparent that her experiences with men had been negative. She was as prickly and defensive as a war survivor, which in a sense she was. What he didn't want was to be joined, in her mind, with the men who had been her enemies in the past.

The slow, patient strategy was working. Now when he kissed her she didn't back off, but opened herself to him. She had even learned to take the lead in kissing, nibbling at his neck or letting her delicate tongue touch his ear in a way that had him squirming with desire.

Each evening, they had relaxed in front of the fireplace, and each time their kisses had taken them into a makeout session that would have put any high school couple to shame.

But he had held himself back from consummating their marriage. Even though she had expressed a willingness, she dreaded it. He felt her fear grow each time they approached the line that separated making out from purposeful foreplay.

And so, each evening, they had taken a walk in the moonlight, and, more important to Gabe, in the cold mountain air that helped him cool the burning desire that threatened to consume him. They'd had wonderful talks about life, and faith, and the stars.

Even with long cold walks, he still had trouble sleeping next to her in the chaste, summer-camp way that they had settled on.

Tonight the walk had scarcely helped at all.

As had happened periodically in the past few days, he flashed on his honeymoon with Melissa. It had been sweet and sunny, not just because of the Caribbean location, but because she had had no barriers to intimacy. But even though he had had free access to her charms, he hadn't felt this kind of dark, dangerous desire. Funny, he thought, crossing his arms behind his head. He was thirty-five, and his physical drives should be less, not more.

Now, as Esperanza finished brushing her hair and walked toward the bed, he couldn't take his eyes off her. But he had to, if he wanted to stay in control. As she slid into bed beside him, he tore his eyes away and stared up at the wooden rafters.

She seemed to sense the difference in his mood. Instead of turning off the bedside lamp she turned to him. "What's wrong, Gabe?" she asked.

He forced himself to keep a light tone. "Nothing. I'm fine. Why?"

"You were awfully quiet tonight. You didn't tell me the name of a single constellation."

"Maybe I told you all of them already."

She reached out and touched his shoulder, tentatively. "Tell me what's wrong."

He turned then to look at her. Newly brushed, her hair looked like black silk spread across her pillow. Her lips were soft and full. Her nightshirt gaped a little at the neck, tempting him to look, to touch.

It took all he had to keep his hands to himself. He didn't have the remaining energy needed to maintain his usual good-natured tone with her. "It's just a little difficult," he ground out, "being with you all day, and kissing you all evening, and getting into bed with you at night, without any ... more."

She bit her lip and her forehead creased with concern.

"It's okay. I told you we could wait until you're ready, and we can. I just can't always act like, you know, a happy kid." He shifted to look at the rafters again. He even started counting them to take his mind off the way her skin seemed to glow in the soft lamplight.

Then she made it worse by scooting over toward him, propping herself on her elbows. "Look," she said slowly. "Whenever it gets too bad, you can, you know, go ahead."

He looked at her then. "What are you saying?"

"When it gets too bad, you can go ahead."

"Esperanza." He sighed. "It's not something I want to do alone, while you just lie there and put up with it. Lovemaking is mutual. It's just an extension of what we've been doing out by the fire every night."

"I don't know when I'll get to that point, where it feels mutual," she said slowly. "You've been great. Better than I would ever have expected a man to be. I just want you to know that when, you know, you can't wait any longer ... it's okay."

The dread in her dark eyes showed him she feared he would

take her up on her offer. But there was courage there, too. She wouldn't back off now that she had made this promise.

But he knew that taking her up on her offer now would cause damage. And despite the desire that threatened to suffocate him, he couldn't bring himself to inflict more damage on her already burdened soul. "We'll wait until you're ready," he said. "Turn off the light. Let's get some sleep."

12

A month after they had returned from their honeymoon and set up housekeeping in the renovated home that had belonged to his grandmother, Gabe was still cranky. It didn't help that everyone seemed to think he should be in a great mood. No one knew he wasn't enjoying the usual benefits of a newlywed man.

And he didn't have very good news to share with Esperanza tonight, either. As he climbed the stairs of their new house into the sunny bird room, he debated how to break it to her.

He had learned to approach the bird room slowly and quietly, and tonight he was glad he did. Esperanza stood illuminated in the setting sun that shone through the window with Paco on her arm. She was talking quietly to the giant bird and feeding him nuts from her hand.

Good—the big guy had calmed down again. The move to a new home had made him revert to his mean ways, and for the first week they'd been back, Esperanza hadn't been able to touch him. Now, slowly, he was regaining his confidence. But this was the first time he'd seen her able to hold him for an extended time.

"You're looking pretty," she crooned softly to Paco. And it was true. Red feathers covered most of his body now; only a few bare spots of skin remained.

Paco wasn't the only one who looked good. Esperanza was her usual, beautiful self, only more so. He thought she'd managed to gain a few pounds since their marriage, and it looked good on her. Her face was more relaxed, and her skin glowed. People had commented to him on how much marriage seemed to agree with Esperanza. There had been some suggestive remarks, too, about why she was glowing.

Looking at her, he knew that the restraint he'd exercised had been the right thing to do. And he hadn't exercised that restraint on his own strength. He'd spent way more time than usual in prayer, in scripture, and at mass.

It was good for his soul, but challenging for his body.

He tapped lightly on the door jamb. "Hey, you two."

Even though his voice was soft, Paco got startled. His big beak opened and he bent as if to bit Esperanza's arm, and Gabe could have kicked himself.

"Don't bite. Kiss," Esperanza said quickly and firmly.

The bird paused. Then he straightened up and bent his head.

Esperanza kissed it. "Good boy!" she exclaimed.

Gabe watched moodily as she placed the bird back on its perch. Even the bird got more affection than he did.

She gave the bird another nut and then came over to Gabe, who still stood in the doorway. "He's making great progress," she said. And then she touched his arm. "Welcome home."

"Thanks." He held himself back from touching her. Maybe it was wrong of him, but he couldn't continue being partially affectionate. To cover up his coldness, he asked, "How's the bird business?"

"Great," she said, as she hopped down the stairs in front of him. "I had two new clients today. And both of them said they'd seen my ads before, and wanted to come see the birds, but they didn't want to come to that neighborhood where I lived." At the bottom of the stairs she turned suddenly so that he halfway ran into her, and she put her arms around him. "Oh, Gabe, it's so wonderful to have a good place for the birds and for my business. I think it's really going to take off. I don't know how to thank you."

He didn't want her gratitude. He wanted her trust and her love. He extricated himself from her arms. "What smells good?" he asked to soften his withdrawal.

"I made spaghetti sauce. That kitchen is great."

Gabe was glad Esperanza so appreciated the little things. But something about it grated on him. He didn't want to feel that he'd lifted her out of poverty, and in return, she would play the role of a good wife, cooking his dinner, asking about his day. He wanted her to appreciate *him*, and them as a couple.

"We can eat whenever." She tugged at his hand. "Come on, come on. Tell me what you found out about our adoption application."

He followed her into the living room and sat beside her on the couch. This time, he didn't pull his hand away. "It's not good news," he said.

"What?" She sobered instantly and met his eyes, and he saw a flash of her old pain and caution. Instantly he regretted his disgruntlement with her new happy confidence. He would a thousand times rather see that in her eyes than the old, dark, pain, no matter how much suffering his hormones had to take.

He squeezed her hand. "It's not that bad. It's just going to take a little longer than we thought."

"Why?"

"Because the Board says there's no way we can speed up our

application. We have to be married for a year before we can adopt a baby."

"A year before we can even apply?"

"We can get a few things going," he explained. "But we can't be actually put in the book the birth mothers look at until we've passed our first anniversary. It's to give couples time to get used to each other, and test out the marriage, before they take on a new responsibility."

"Can't you bend the rules?"

He shook his head. "No, and after talking to the Chairman of the Board, I wouldn't even try to. It's a good idea."

"Why didn't you tell me it would take that long? Did you know about this?" she demanded, sounding angry.

"I said it would be a year but I'd hoped to get it done sooner. Does it matter so much?"

"Oh, I guess not." She flopped back on the couch, not meeting his eyes. "I just want to get on with it, you know?"

"Is it so bad, just being with me?" he asked. Then, immediately, he regretted the question.

"Uh . . . no. No, of course not."

But it was. Gabe could read it in her eyes, and it just cemented what had been bothering him from the moment he'd come home, and indeed for the past two weeks.

Esperanza was grateful for what he could provide. She would be especially grateful when their status as a couple allowed them to adopt. But she didn't really care for him. She would be glad when there was a baby or two to break the tension between them.

∽

Esperanza was relieved when Gabe finished eating. She whipped his plate away the moment he'd taken his last bite. She hadn't been able to eat much, herself.

She knew she had reacted childishly about the delay in adopting babies, but she couldn't help herself. It seemed like the millionth time she'd had to put her dream on hold.

And there was another more compelling reason she wanted to adopt a baby now. It would help take the focus on her and Gabe as a couple.

Oh, she'd been playing happy and content. In fact, much of it wasn't an act. She genuinely loved the home and the things he provided. More than that, her heart leapt when she heard his step on the stairs. When he walked into a room her whole world lit up.

But that was dangerous, because it was apparent he didn't feel the same about her. She badly needed an outlet for the love she had to give, because she didn't dare expend it all on Gabe.

He'd given her clear enough signals. When she touched him, he pulled away. When she hugged him, he just put up with it for a moment, and then actually took her arms from around him.

He had been so wonderful, so patient and kind, on their honeymoon, that she kept wishing they could have that time back. Now, he didn't spend an hour kissing and talking with her each evening. He brought a book to bed, read late into the night, and then turned his back on her and went to sleep.

She scraped the remains of her dinner into the garbage disposal, and then put the plate into the dishwasher, purposely taking pleasure in the appliances that made cleaning up so easy. She should be happy. She had more than she'd ever expected to have. And she wasn't going to ruin it by demanding that Gabe love her back.

"Let me help with that," he said, coming up behind her.

"It's okay. It's easy," she said.

"Two can do it faster than one."

"What's the rush?"

"Actually," Gabe said, "I think my family might come over tonight."

Esperanza froze, a glass halfway in the dishwasher. "You're kidding. The whole family?"

"Well... Mom, Bianca, maybe John. Why? Is that bad?"

"I haven't got everything clean—"

"That's why I'm offering to help," he said.

"No, I mean, really clean. I need to straighten up the family room, and sweep the bird room—"

"Relax," he said. "It's just family. They don't expect everything to be perfect."

But she couldn't help rushing around trying to clean up their already-clean house. Gabe's family, or at least his mother, was on the lookout for things to criticize about her. She didn't want to give them that satisfaction.

The moment she opened the door to find not only Gabe's mother, and Bianca, and John, but also the snarky Nicola, she knew it was going to be a bad night. Mrs. Montana had the glazed look that told Esperanza that she had taken too many of her pills. This was something, she was beginning to realize, that happened regularly. At the wedding she had chalked it up to nerves, but in the month they'd been back from the honeymoon, she had realized that the woman was out of it most of the time. She had mentioned it to Gabe, but he had been so surprised and dismissive that she hadn't pushed the issue.

Just as Esperanza expected, Mrs. Montana started complaining before she'd taken off her coat. While Gabe was busy opening the door to Bianca and John, she sniffed the air delicately. "It's awfully garlicky in here," she said, her words slightly slurred. "Are you cooking up quaint ethnic meals for Gabriel?"

"If spaghetti's quaint and ethnic, I guess I am." She tried to sound pleasant, although this whole visit had caught her off-guard. "Why don't you come on into the living room. Would you like some coffee?" Maybe that would sober the woman up.

"Why, certainly. You know," she said, leaning close to Esperanza, "Melissa always used to have something sweet ready after dinner. But I don't imagine you have time for much baking, what with all of your business concerns."

"I can see why she wanted to sweeten you up," Esperanza muttered under her breath as she turned and almost ran to the kitchen.

She talked to herself while she filled the coffee pot and dug up a bag of store-bought sugar cookies. *You can't change her, so don't even try. It's the pills talking. Even if she means it personally, it doesn't do any good to take it personally.*

By the time the coffee had finished dripping, Esperanza had herself a little more together, but she still felt shaky. She was going to talk to Gabe about giving her more advance warning about these visits. She was going to rise above Mrs. Montana's digs. She was going to focus on Bianca and John, the parts of his family that she truly liked, and keep a polite distance from the rest of them.

At least, that was what she thought until she walked toward the living room, tray in hand, only to hear Mrs. Montana's loud, slurring voice.

"I'm not surprised about the delay in adoption proceedings," she said. "They'll need some time to check out her background. The Lord only knows what she's been into."

Mrs. Montana was talking to Nicola, while Gabe was over by the television talking with John. Maybe he hadn't heard? But

Bianca, who was across the room, looked upset—so she had obviously heard Mrs. Montana's remarks.

Esperanza pushed down her own worries about background checks. Juvenile records were closed, and anyway, Mrs. Montana knew nothing of her past. She was just making her usual ugly assumptions.

"They'll be lucky to get any child, let alone a white baby. They might have to settle for some drug addicted—"

"Hey." Esperanza strode in and set the tray down on the coffee table with a little bang. She faced her mother in law, hands on hips. "It's not *my* background check I'm worried about. I'm sure the agency will want some reassurances that we won't leave the child alone with a grandmother who's hooked on pills."

There was a frozen silence. Everyone stared at Esperanza. "You mean ... Mom? Hooked on pills?" Bianca said softly.

Esperanza didn't take her eyes off Mrs. Montana. "I hope the pills are the reason she's acting this way."

The older woman looked away, her hands fluttering to her face. "I never heard anything so rude," she sputtered. "Gabriel, are you going to allow your wife to speak to me like that?"

Esperanza turned to Gabe, eyebrows raised, wondering about his reaction.

He certainly didn't jump to her defense. "Look, Eppie," he began, his voice low, "she doesn't ..."

"Of all the nerve," interrupted Nicola. "I knew you were from a street background, Esperanza, but you have to stop looking at things that way now. Addicts are in your world, not ours."

"Mom's got some medical problems," said Bianca, "but that's the only pills she takes."

Esperanza backed toward the door. She was under attack from all sides, and she knew she couldn't win. Best to beat a strategic retreat. "You guys enjoy the coffee," she said, waving her hand toward the tray. "I think I'll... check on the birds."

As she walked away, she heard Mrs. Montana start to whine. "I can't tolerate that kind of abuse," she said.

"It's okay, Mom."

"Don't worry about her. She doesn't know what she's talking about."

Esperanza shook her head and then ran up the stairs. What a sick family. But even knowing she was right, it still hurt to have all of them against her. Especially Gabe.

GABE DID damage control as best he could, but he was seething. He didn't argue when Bianca suggested that they all should leave, that she was sure Gabe had an early morning tomorrow.

The truth was, he couldn't wait for them to be gone so that he could confront Esperanza about what she had said.

"Don't be too hard on her, Gabe," Bianca whispered, having hung back behind the others. "Mom *was* being nasty to her. You didn't hear the things she said."

"That's no excuse for that kind of accusation," Gabe said.

Bianca shrugged. "Think how it would be to come new into a family like this," she advised. "Put yourself in her shoes for a minute." And then, as their mother's querulous voice rang out from the car, Bianca waved and hurried toward her.

As Gabe headed up the stairs where Esperanza had disappeared almost an hour ago, he let Bianca's advice slow him down. It was true, their mother was always blunt and often rude. The family was accustomed to it; it was partly the physical pain caused by her arthritis, partly the result of the loss of their father at an early age, and then of Melissa and her only grandchild. Esperanza probably didn't know the full story.

He still felt annoyed, but he took some deep breaths. He would try to be reasonable.

He met Esperanza coming out of the bird room. Her eyes were a little red, but she tossed her hair back with an angry gesture. For a moment they looked at one another without saying anything.

Then they both started speaking at once.

"I hope you've done some thinking about—" Gabe began.

"Thanks a lot for leaping to my defense—" Esperanza snarled.

They both stopped and glared at each other.

"Thanks a lot for standing up for me," Esperanza repeated. "You know, Gabe, I realize you're attached to your family. But like it or not, I'm your wife. You need to stand up for me when I'm obviously right, like tonight."

"Obviously right? Are you out of your mind?"

She stared at him, her expression blank. "You mean . . . you don't realize I was right?"

"Right to humiliate an old, sick woman in front of her entire family?"

Esperanza crossed her arms over her chest. "So . . . she can humiliate me, make degrading remarks about my background, my abilities, my roots, and even my morality, and that's fine? But I can't call her on her addiction?"

Gabe shook his head slowly back and forth. "She is *not* addicted to anything. She takes pain pills for her arthritis, yes. But they're prescribed by her doctor."

"I don't think so, Gabe. She talks and acts like an addict."

"You're letting your own background color your view of her," he said angrily. "She's a little too outspoken, yes. But we've all learned to make allowances because of all she's been through."

"Lots of people have been through bad experiences, Gabe.

Some of them turn into better people because of it. Suffering isn't a good reason to put other people down."

They were standing at the top of the stairs, virtually hissing at one another. How incongruous that in the middle of it, Gabe should notice that they were right next to their bedroom. And that Esperanza, in her semi-tight jeans and with her eyes flashing brown fire, looked incredibly attractive.

He got a sudden, cave-man impulse to throw her over his shoulder and take her to bed. To show her who was boss. To get that cocky, angry expression off her face, to soften those eyes and lips to the look of love.

"What?" she said. "I'm right, aren't I?"

He crossed his arms over his chest and looked away from her, buying time. For one thing, he had no idea what the question was. For another, he was mad at himself for coming up with the ridiculous notion of taking her to bed. For pity's sake, he'd never once had that privilege, even though they'd been married for over a month now, even though she felt perfectly free to criticize his family like any shrewish wife.

"Well? Don't you see I'm right?"

"No."

"You're driving me crazy." She shook her head and turned to go down the stairs.

He didn't know what it was that made him touch her shoulder, then grip it. She turned back, her eyes questioning, and he moved closer to her, gripping her other shoulder.

Instantly she twisted away from him, teetering precariously close to the top of the stairs. Gabe stepped forward and pulled her back, surrounding her with his arms. His heart was pounding. No matter how ridiculous and irrational she was, he didn't want to lose her. It was his *job* to protect her.

"Let go of me!" She tried to twist away.

He held on to her. "Calm down."

"Let go!" There was genuine panic in her flailing now.

He moved so that his body blocked the top of the stairs and let her go. As soon as she was free she moved as far away as possible.

"Don't you *ever* do that again."

"Do what?" Gabe was trying to cope with how much her nearness had aroused him. He could barely think.

"Hold me like that. Restrain me."

"I didn't want you to fall down the stairs."

She watched him, her eyes narrow. "Yeah, right. They all have some excuse." And then she spun into the bedroom and slammed the door.

Gabe heard the lock click.

Leaning back against the railing at the top of the stairs, Gabe caught his breath, willing his body to calm down. He had married the most exasperating woman in the world. Esperanza was ready to take offense at the drop of a hat, whether it was his mother's careless remarks or his own efforts to save her from physical harm.

He thought briefly, longingly, of Melissa. Melissa, who had never fought with him over *anything*. Who had catered to his mother's every mood.

Who had never aroused him like this.

At that realization, Gabe gripped the banister tightly. He didn't want to think it. It seemed like sacrilege that this impulsive, uptight, annoying woman could take him places the angelic Melissa hadn't known existed.

It was *really* sick that he'd never even slept with Esperanza.

Gabe stared at the closed bedroom door. Any normal pair of newlyweds who'd had a fight at least had the pleasure of making up. Lovemaking was a way to heal the little wounds that inevitably came up as two very different people adjusted to one another.

He should break down that door and force her to make up, kiss away her fears, love away that angry, prickly, defensive part of her.

But then he remembered the panicked fear in her eyes when she had thought he was restraining her. No matter how much he wanted to, he wasn't going to be the cause of more fear.

Gabe clenched his jaw and turned away from the closed door. It looked like he'd sleep on the couch tonight.

13

"So what's bugging you?" Rhonda asked as she opened the car window, seemingly oblivious to the chilly March air that rushed in.

"Nothing," Esperanza snapped, steering the car into the bumper-to-bumper freeway traffic, "except that I'm freezing."

"Really? Geez, I'm so hot. This pregnancy thing is weird." But Rhonda raised the window most of the way. "It's so great Gabe got you this car."

"Uh-huh," Esperanza said without enthusiasm. Her small hatchback had died, and Gabe had insisted on buying her a brand-new sports sedan. Another reason to feel obligated to him, and guilty about the fact that they were now barely speaking.

Not to mention the guilt she felt over the fact that she now had so much and Rhonda so little. "You know, I could give you the money to see a doctor in town. There's no reason we have to go this far to a free clinic."

"The reason is, it's what I can afford. But I sure appreciate the ride. The bus takes hours, and it's not nearly this comfortable." Rhonda leaned back in the leather seat, sighing with pleasure. "Anyway, this gives us a chance to talk. How's married life?"

"Don't ask."

Rhonda turned toward her. "Uh-oh. What's going wrong?"

Esperanza shrugged. "It's no big deal," she said. And it wasn't, compared to the problems Rhonda had: an unplanned pregnancy, unreliable boyfriend, and a boss who wasn't sympathetic to her need for monthly checkups.

"Tell me anyway," Rhonda said.

So Esperanza briefly described the family visit the previous night and its culmination in the fight with Gabe.

"I'm not surprised about the witch on wheels," Rhonda said. "But I *am* surprised that Gabe puts up with her. He seems like a fair guy, usually."

"Yes, well, not where his mom's concerned."

Rhonda shrugged. "It'll blow over," she said. "Don't worry about it."

"Easier said than done," Esperanza muttered as she exited the parkway.

Rhonda sat up and looked around, pointed in the direction of the clinic, and then studied Esperanza with interest. "Why's this little fight got you so upset?" she asked. "You've got everything you want. Adoption proceedings started. A great new home. The bird business is going great. So Gabe's a little stressed about his family. Just let it roll off you. He'll get over it."

"I guess," Esperanza said, pulling into the clinic's parking lot. Rhonda was right, of course. Her life had improved by leaps and bounds. It was almost a Cinderella story.

But the prince was angry at her, and Cinderella felt miserable about it.

As she followed Rhonda into the clinic's enormous waiting room, she pondered why Gabe's anger so bothered her. She'd had every right to be angry last night, and she still felt his mother had been awful to her.

But she could also understand having blind spots where one's family was concerned. She'd definitely overlooked plenty of problems in Rhonda in the past few years, just because Rhonda was the closest thing to a sister that she had.

She understood Gabe's protectiveness toward his mother. And she hated it that he was angry with her. Because...

Because she loved him.

Rhonda must have seen the surprised expression on her face. "What's up, sis?" she asked as she lowered herself into a chair. "You look like you just saw a big old spider or something."

"I just... figured something out, and I don't like it," she said.

"So spill it. It looks like we've got nearly an hour wait, so we might as well talk."

Esperanza groaned. "I think I'm in love with him, Rhonda."

Rhonda cocked her head to one side. "With who?"

"With Gabe, you crazy girl. Who else?"

"Oh. So what's the problem?"

"The problem is," Esperanza said, "he's mad at me, his family's mad at me, and he doesn't love me back."

"How do you know that?"

Esperanza shook her head rapidly. "I just know it. He still thinks about Melissa. He still has a picture of her in his office. Oh, sure, he put up a wedding picture of us as well, but that was for show. Marrying me was a... sort of a charity case for Gabe."

"What about how he can't keep his eyes off you whenever you two are together?" Rhonda asked. "Doesn't that mean he cares? He watches you like a hawk."

"That's something else," Esperanza said.

"Which is..."

Esperanza rolled up the magazine she'd been toying with and started slapping her palm with it. "That's just... desire."

Rhonda looked amused. "Just desire, huh? Well, if that's the case, it should have burned out by now. Believe me, honey, once a guy has satisfied that initial urge, he won't come back unless he cares for you at least a little."

Esperanza stared down at the magazine, feeling her face redden. What Rhonda didn't know—what nobody knew—was that Gabe hadn't had the opportunity to satisfy that initial urge. That she was still, after more than a month of marriage, a virgin bride.

The door leading to the back of the clinic opened, and, half-hidden behind the door, a med-tech called out a name. Esperanza jumped at the sound of the voice and stared at Rhonda, who was staring back at her.

"Did that sound like Wayne to you?" Esperanza asked.

Rhonda nodded slowly. "Sure did. But it couldn't be. Did you see his face?"

Esperanza shook her head. "I couldn't see him."

"It couldn't be," Rhonda repeated. "You said he was back in town, but what would Wayne the Psycho be doing in a free clinic?"

Esperanza shook her head. "His scrubs looked like a tech."

"He was always good at science and stuff."

"It really did sound like him, didn't it? And I told you he's back in the city." Of course, Esperanza had told Rhonda about her recent encounter with Wayne.

The door opened again, and they snapped to attention. This time there was no mistaking it. Rhonda quickly turned away from the man and Esperanza lifted her magazine in front of her face, and another woman answered the summons and headed for the clinic's inner door.

"Come on," Esperanza said, "let's get out of here."

"What about my appointment?"

"You're not keeping an appointment at a clinic where Wayne works."

Rhonda stood slowly. "You've got a point. No way am I getting anywhere near one of those hospital gowns with him in the building."

When they heard the inner door open again, their urge to run was mutual and instinctual. They hustled out of the clinic door without any explanation to the receptionist.

Out on the street, they stared at each other. Esperanza felt disoriented, thrown back to the same state of mind she'd had in that rattletrap house with Wayne and too many other kids with too little adult supervision.

"Come on," Rhonda said, grabbing her arm, "you can't drive. Let's go get a cup of coffee, maybe some dinner." She pulled Esperanza in the direction of a nondescript little restaurant.

"What if he comes in here?" Esperanza asked at the door.

"He can't do anything to us," Rhonda said reasonably. "If he tries, we can call the police."

"All right, but let's sit in the back."

They sat for at least an hour, drinking tea, barely talking. Finally, Rhonda ordered food for both of them—Esperanza didn't pay attention to what—and then leaned back in the padded booth, staring up at the ceiling. "What is that clinic thinking, hiring a jerk like that to work with women?"

"Someone should tell them. We should tell them."

"Tell them what? That he can't keep his hands to himself?" Rhonda laughed bitterly. "Who would believe us?"

"That stuff ought to be on his record. From . . . you know, that one time."

It was something they never talked about, the most horrific night of both their lives.

Rhonda met Esperanza's eyes, shaking her head. "I don't

think so. You were both minors, and anyway, the charges were against you, not him."

"And then they were dropped. When people found out what really happened."

"Uh-huh. But there's no record about why, most likely. Anyway, they close the records on minors, I think."

Their food arrived. Rhonda dug in, and Esperanza pushed hers around on the plate. For several moments they didn't speak.

"We should still call the clinic," Esperanza said finally. "Sure, we can't talk specifically about that time, but he's probably done other things since then. And even if he hasn't, the least we can do is warn his co-workers to keep an eye on him around the patients."

"We could do that," Rhonda said, nodding and chewing. "I have the clinic number."

"Give it to me. I'm calling right now."

Her heart pounding, Esperanza made the call. The receptionist who answered sounded disbelieving, as if this were nothing but a prank, but Esperanza urged her to check out his background and keep an eye on him. Finally, when the receptionist's voice sounded more interested, Esperanza hung up.

"Good job," Rhonda said. "I ordered us chocolate cake. We deserve it."

Again Rhonda ate and Esperanza picked. "I wish there were more we could do," Esperanza said, when they'd finally pulled themselves together enough to head back home.

"Well, there's not, so just forget about him," Rhonda said. "And . . . I think I might take you up on that offer of your helping me find a doctor in town."

A Bond of Hope

GABE HAD ARRIVED home from work to an empty house. He and Esperanza hadn't spoken in the morning—he'd gotten up from the couch early and headed for work, avoiding her—so he didn't know her plans. But as the evening stretched out longer and she didn't return, he got worried.

He called the old house, where Rhonda was still living, but there was no answer. That didn't reassure him. They were probably together, which meant that Eppie could be getting into all sorts of trouble. He had grown to like Rhonda somewhat, but he didn't trust her judgement. Even though she seemed to have quieted down since she'd gotten pregnant, he could easily imagine her dragging Esperanza out to some bar. There they would share their tales of woe about men, and probably meet plenty more who were willing to offer comfort... and a whole lot more.

He shook off that thought. Esperanza and Bianca had become better friends in the past month. Maybe she'd gone to his sister's house to talk about last night's disastrous visit. He dialed Bianca's number and asked if Esperanza was there.

"Nope, I haven't seen her," Bianca said. "Why? Don't you know where she is?"

"She usually leaves a note, but she didn't today."

"Let me ask Mom and Nicola if they know anything."

"Wait—" But it was too late. *Wonderful*, Gabe thought. Let's just give them more things to poke at Esperanza about.

Throughout the day he'd grown increasingly ashamed of his attitude toward his wife. Bianca's words had hit home. What would his family look like from the outside? They all knew to make allowances for their mother, but Esperanza didn't know her whole history. To top that off, his mother's losses paled in comparison to Esperanza's own troubled past. Yet Esperanza was unfailingly kind to others, nothing like the rude, overbearing woman his mother had become.

It made sense that his mother's remarks, digging just at Esperanza's sensitivities, had pierced Esperanza's usual kindness and made her snap. And the conclusion she'd jumped to—that his mother had a drug problem—wasn't that outlandish given what she was used to.

"They don't know where she is either," Bianca reported at the same moment that Gabe heard Esperanza's key in the door.

"I think I hear her," Gabe said. A moment later Esperanza walked into the kitchen. He put his hand over the mouthpiece of the phone. "Where have you been?" he hissed.

"I took Rhonda to the North Side Free Clinic," she said.

A clinic. Not, then, a bar. He uncovered the phone. "Yes, she's home. False alarm. She was taking Rhonda to the North Side Free Clinic and . . . they must have run into some delays. Tell everyone, will you?"

After he'd hung up he leaned back against the counter. He didn't trust himself to start speaking, because he was afraid he'd accuse her and start another fight. That was the last thing they needed.

She didn't say anything either. She walked past him, and he heard her opening the hall closet, hanging up her coat. Then she went into the living room.

He followed and sat down across from her. Was she going to be silent forever? And why was she so pale? Her dark eyes looked enormous, her face drawn, and dark circles were obvious under her eyes.

"Are you okay?" he finally asked, gruffly.

She nodded. "Who was on the phone?"

"Bianca," he said. "I was worried about you. I was calling around to see if anyone knew where you were."

"I took Rhonda to the clinic in the city," she said. "We . . . had a couple of delays. I didn't expect to be so late."

"Is everything okay?"

He could have sworn that she was going to cry. Those dark windows of pain were wide open in her eyes. In a second he was on the couch beside her. "Honey, what is it? Is Rhonda going to be okay?"

She nodded quickly. "She's fine. It's just . . ." She looked at him searchingly. Whatever she was thinking about telling him, he saw the moment when she changed her mind. "Nothing."

"You're my wife. You need to tell me what's wrong so I can fix it."

She gave him an odd look."Some things can't be fixed, Gabe."

"Try me."

She shook her head. "We had an irritating experience at the clinic, that's all. I'd like to try to find Rhonda a doctor here in town."

"Good idea," he said. "She'll get better care here. And that clinic's not in a very good neighborhood, is it?"

"Free clinics usually aren't." She picked at a loose thread in the sofa cushion. "So," she said without looking up, "I guess you're not mad at me anymore? Or not *as* mad, anyway?"

The hurt in her voice made him want to soothe her pain. "I did some thinking today," he said. "I should have been more understanding last night. I'm sorry I yelled at you."

She looked up at him through a fringe of long dark hair. "I'm sorry too. I know a little bit about feeling protective when it comes to your family."

They looked at each other for a long moment. Then he reached out to wrap an arm around her shoulder. Suddenly the air shimmered between them with hope, a possibility of reconciliation. "Eppie," he said softly, "there's something else going on too."

"Yeah?" She went back to picking at the sofa thread, but he could tell she was listening.

"Yeah." He paused, wondering how much to say, and how to phrase it. Once he'd apologized about yelling, it seemed like his false pride was gone.

And yes, his machismo was threatened by the fact that he wasn't bedding his wife. But he knew her fear was still alive and well.

"Well?" she asked finally, looking up at him as she tucked her hair behind one ear. "Are you going to tell me what? Or do you want me to start guessing?"

"Um." He decided to just plunge ahead and forget about eloquence. "I'm having trouble living with you this way," he said quickly. "I have certain needs . . ." He trailed off, trying to read her eyes, thinking maybe he'd said just the wrong thing.

"Needs." Her expression was unreadable.

"Uh-huh. Physical needs. And not just physical," he added hastily. "I . . . well, I'd like to be closer to you in every way."

"You want sex," she said flatly.

He sighed. "When you put it like that, it sounds so shallow. It's not just sex, it's closeness. Intimacy. Like last night. If we were sleeping together, we could have made up then, instead of going through the whole night and day angry." He touched her chin. "We could have *both* gotten some sleep."

"Gabe, I told you. When you feel like you need to, just ask. I'm your wife. I . . . know my obligations." Meanwhile, her eyes begged him. *Not tonight, please not tonight.*

He shook his head slowly. "You just don't get it, do you? If it's done right, lovemaking isn't an obligation. It's a precious gift."

"Hmmm."

He blundered on. "All I'm saying is, let's move in that direction, okay? It doesn't have to be tonight, if we don't want to. But I can't take this marital chastity much longer."

"All right," she said so softly he could barely hear her.

He pulled her closer, felt her stiffen, and settled for a kiss on the head. "Come on. While I was worrying about where you were, I made some chili. Let's have a little dinner."

~

THAT NIGHT ESPERANZA hesitated in front of her chest of drawers, listening to the sound of Gabe whistling in the shower. She opened her pajama drawer and pawed past the flannel sleep shirts to the tissue-wrapped delicacies beneath.

Between Rhonda and Bianca, she'd received as wedding gifts several silky nightgowns that she'd been afraid to wear so far. She'd tried them on and seen how they transformed her from girlish to sensual and womanly. It was a transformation that frightened her. And she didn't want to entice Gabe unfairly if she couldn't follow through.

Still, it was as he said. He wasn't going to be able to tolerate this type of life forever. He'd been far more patient than most men would ever be. And they had to start somewhere.

She heard the shower turn off. Before she could lose her nerve, she pulled out the least revealing of the nightgowns. Its red silk set off her dark skin and hair, and its short, plain style suited her. She slipped it on and started folding up her clothes, then sat down in front of her mirror to brush her hair.

When he came in she looked up and saw his reflection in the mirror. So she caught the way he froze and drew in his breath.

Their eyes met in the mirror. Esperanza gave her already-shiny hair two more strokes.

In a minute that seemed to take forever he crossed the room to stand behind her, still watching her face in the mirror. "Do you know," he asked, "just how breathtakingly beautiful you look?"

Esperanza felt her cheeks redden. To take the focus off herself, she looked at him, dressed only in pajama bottoms, at his wide shoulders, his muscular arms, his large, capable hands. "You don't look bad yourself," she murmured.

He reached out and took the brush from her hand. Slowly, gently, he started brushing her hair for her.

It wasn't the move she expected. As he continued, she let her eyes close and concentrated on the feel of his hands as he stroked her face, her head, her shoulders. It felt like caretaking of the kind she'd never had enough of, and as it went on she let her head fall back against his flat stomach.

Slowly she realized he wasn't using the brush anymore, but was running his hands through her hair, down her shoulders and arms. The warm, slightly rough feel of his hands on her skin made her heart pound, and she didn't know if what she felt was excitement or fear.

And then, as he squatted down behind her, she caught sight of her face in the mirror. Her eyes, half-closed, lips full, parted slightly; hair spilling loose across her shoulders. She wasn't used to looking at herself in the mirror at all, let alone in this condition, wearing red silk. She turned to bury her face on Gabe's shoulder.

His arms were around her instantly, comforting, soothing. "Hey," he whispered. "Are you okay?"

She nodded, still feeling somehow embarrassed.

"Come to bed," he said.

She lifted her face and stared at him. Did he mean what she thought he meant? Was this the time?

He sank back on his heels so that he was looking up at her. "Esperanza. Do you trust me? Do you trust me not to hurt you?"

Gabe held his breath.

Esperanza hesitated, then spoke. "I trust you," she said slowly, "to *try* to be gentle. As gentle as a man can be."

He stood, pulled her to her feet, and drew her toward the bed. "Tonight's not about me. Tonight, it's all about you."

14

The next day Esperanza sang as she cared for the birds and blushed while she prepared dinner, thinking of how she had forgotten her modesty under the strange miracles Gabe had worked on her last night.

She hadn't known such feelings existed. Always before when people—like Rhonda—did foolish things for the sake of romantic attraction, she had thought they were crazy. Now, her body imprinted with Gabe's exhilarating touch, she almost understood.

Her contentment stemmed from something more than the physical pleasure, too. She had seen the desire in his eyes, had felt it when he lay close beside her. She had never known a man who would hold back in that situation. In fact, she remembered several instances where boys or men acted as if their arousal was her fault and thus her responsibility to relieve.

Gabe had restrained himself. Even when she'd offered, he had held back. He might not be in love with her, but that sacrifice showed real caring. And it gave her confidence that, when they did take their love to full fruition, he would be kind enough to go slowly.

She was just chopping the last of the salad vegetables when she heard Gabe's car pull up, and her heart leapt inside her. He'd come home early. Maybe he was just as affected by last night as she was.

But when he burst through the door and strode heavily down the hall, Esperanza got a foreboding of something bad about to happen. When he appeared in the kitchen, there was thunder in his voice and lightning in his eyes. And his sister Nicola was right behind him with a smug expression that made Esperanza wary.

"Why didn't you tell me the whole story about your past?" he demanded.

Esperanza's heart took a sudden guilty jump and she backed up to the kitchen counter, gripping it with both hands as she faced him. "What do you mean?"

He looked at her as if she were a convicted criminal, shaking his head, and then turned to his sister and propelled her forward. "Tell her what you told me. What you told the whole agency."

Nicola shrugged from beneath his hand and rubbed her shoulder. "Don't shoot the messenger. I just thought you should know what I found out. And I thought the adoption agency should know too, because it might influence their decision about your adoption."

"You were right about that, if it's true," Gabe said grimly.

"Excuse me," Esperanza said, hearing the unnatural highness of her voice. "Could somebody let me in on the big secret?"

Nicola sneered at her. "You're the one with the secret. It's lucky Mom thought of talking to her friends on the Board of Trustees of Cleveland's Foster Care Program. Otherwise, we might never have known about how you got arrested. For assaulting another kid. And slapped in the juvenile detention center." She sniffed, her nose wrinkling as if she'd encountered a bad smell. "As if someone with a history like that could adopt a child. As if someone like that should be a part of *our* family."

Esperanza's knees turned to jelly. She gripped the counter as hard as she could and closed her eyes for a moment.

So it was over. It was out. The secret she had tried so hard to erase from her own mind, as well as from the records that any adoption home study would be likely to look at. It was the main reason she'd settled on Open Arms; the previous director had assured her that they didn't try to uncover juvenile records, that they considered everyone with a clean slate at eighteen.

Of course, the previous director had been corrupt, and Gabe, honorable Gabe, was changing all that.

When she opened her eyes and looked at Gabe, she felt like crying. All the warmth and caring was gone from his face.

"So it's true," he said slowly. "Even while we were driving over here, I had some hope . . . "

Esperanza took a deep breath and started fighting for her life, the life she was trying to build for herself, the life she wanted. "Hold on. Did you know that the charges were dropped after a couple of days? That there was never an official charge?"

Gabe nodded, his eyes still icy. "We know. It's all in the documents Nicola somehow got her vindictive little hands on."

"Gabe!" Nicola's voice was a whine.

He ignored her. "But if you were innocent," he said to Esperanza, "then it's strange that you spent the next three months in the juvenile detention center. Under maximum security."

Put like that, it sounded bad. "Gabe, it was a very complicated situation. I'd like to explain it to you, but it's going to take awhile. Let's sit down, at least." She moved toward the kitchen table.

"Oh, we've heard the long explanation," Nicola said. "From the kid you assaulted. Mom figured we should get it from the horses' mouth, and when we heard about your trip with that foster sister of yours to the clinic where he works, we knew we were onto something."

"You . . . you talked to Wayne?" Esperanza staggered and had to grab the kitchen table for support. Slowly, carefully, she lowered herself into a chair.

"See?" Nicola said triumphantly to Gabe. "She knows the game's over now."

"Nicola," Gabe said, his voice deadly, "why don't you get out."

Esperanza looked up in time to see Nicola's hurt surprise. "Fine. You're the one who wanted me to come over, though. Remember that." She started to huff away.

"Nicola." Esperanza heard how her own voice sounded as if she'd been running a great distance. "Wait a minute. Did you tell Wayne where I live? Or where Rhonda lives?"

"Uh," Nicola said. "I might have. Why? Scared he's going to come tell more of the ugly details?"

Esperanza didn't answer. She just let her head drop into her hand as she felt the last shards of the life she'd built crash down around her.

After a minute she heard Nicola's heels clicking down the hallway. The front door slammed. A car started.

Then, silence.

When she finally looked up at Gabe, he was staring out the kitchen window. She hated the expression on his face. He looked so . . . betrayed.

Guilt settled in her chest, a heavy weight. "Gabe . . . I don't know where to start."

He turned to study her face. Then he said, "How about you start by telling me why, in all the time we were dating and talking about marriage and adopting kids, you never thought to mention this . . . this little . . . *event* in your past."

She nodded slowly. "That was wrong. I'm so sorry, Gabe. I should have told you."

"Yes, you should have. Can I ask why you didn't?"

"I just . . . I don't know how to explain it. For one thing, it's not exactly my proudest moment. And I thought the records were closed."

"You thought you wouldn't get caught." He crossed his arms over his chest.

"Gabe, I wasn't in the wrong, or not totally. I can explain what happened if you want to hear it." Even as she said it, the bile rose in her throat, thinking of the night she'd tried so hard to forget.

But if she had to resurrect it, for Gabe's sake, she would.

He seemed to read her reluctance. "Just tell me one thing. Did you attack this kid with a knife? Or, if I can put it more exactly . . . " He pulled an official looking document from the folder Nicola had thrown on the windowsill. "Did you attack Wayne Little with an unregistered switchblade, causing permanent scarring to his facial features?"

The whole, horrible nightmare came back to her then. A boy far bigger than she was, bigger and more powerful and more entitled, who knew he had his parents and the authorities on his side because he belonged to the family, while she was just a foster child.

Now, as then, she struck out angrily. "Yeah, I did, okay? I pulled out the blade I bought off a kid on the street the day before. And when I clicked it out, he was scared. For once he was scared—of *me*."

She paused to make sure Gabe was listening, and thought she caught an echo of Wayne's mixed fear and horror in Gabe's eyes. Anger surged through her.

"It felt *good*, Gabe. It felt good to cut him."

He slammed the folder shut. "Okay. That's all I need to know." He dropped it on the table as he crossed the room toward the door.

She was shaking, but some shred of common sense told her not to leave the story there. "There's more to it," she said hoarsely. "What's that file, anyway? Did you read the whole thing?"

His eyes froze her. "It only gets worse. 3-month incarceration, with solitary confinement and the occasional need for physical restraint."

"Did you read why I attacked him?"

"Unprovoked. That's what the report says." He sighed. "Look, I didn't like Wayne when we saw him on the street, and I didn't like what I heard about him from Mom and Nicola. But the report corroborates his story."

"So of course you believe it."

He went on as if he hadn't heard her. "Nothing we planned can happen now. I don't understand why you did this. I don't know what I've married." He walked out of the room, his heavy strides echoed loudly in the hallway and then on the stairs.

Esperanza stared at the ceiling, blinking back tears. *I don't know what I've married.* Not even *who*, but *what*. Like she was some horrible freak of nature, lower than pond scum. Like she wasn't a person at all.

After a long time she picked up the file Gabe had dropped and leafed through it, listlessly. What on earth was it? Obviously Gabe had been mislead, whether by Nicola, his mother, Wayne, or some corrupt official in the foster care system she didn't know. The attack had been most heavily provoked, and in self-defense. The charges had been dropped after the whole story had come out. The switchblade was a mistake she regretted—and paid for—every day of her life.

She put her head down on the table. She didn't cry; her grief was too new and too deep for tears.

Open Arms had been her last chance of adopting children, and now that they knew her history, they would never approve her. She already knew whose version of the story they would believe. Gabe—who supposedly cared for her—had just demonstrated that when it came down to a controversy, he'd believe the official story, or Wayne's version, over her own. And why should she be surprised? That was always the way it had always been.

Her dream was dead.

And how cruel that now, now when she had just realized how deeply she loved Gabe, she had completely lost his trust.

She didn't know how long she sat there. How could she measure time when the clock by which she had measured her life had broken? What did it matter, now, what she did?

As if in mockery, the kitchen clock on the wall ticked loudly, invading her cocoon of misery. She turned her head to the side to look at it, and a sudden stabbing pain pierced her heart, worse than the ache that was already there.

The clock was a gift from Gabe. A silly gift, a joke, because they'd agreed they wouldn't buy each other wedding presents. But he had seen the tacky clock shaped like a parrot's head and hadn't been able to resist it. She'd hooted with laughter when she saw it, and had put it up in the kitchen as soon as they'd moved in.

The card that accompanied it—also parrot-shaped—had read, in Gabe's nearly-unreadable scrawl, "Minutes, hours, days, years. I look forward to the future with you."

That was before their wonderful honeymoon, before the past awkward month. Last night, their future together had again looked hopeful and bright.

And now, he didn't know *what* he'd married.

She drew her legs up into the chair and wrapped her arms around them, trying to pray. But the clock's irritating *tick-tock* wouldn't leave her alone.

She should *never* have let herself grow to care about Gabe. She should have seen it happening and taken measures to distance herself. Caring, getting close, trusting someone—all it led to was this ripping, agonizing severance, this hole in the heart.

The knees of her jeans were wet where she'd rested her closed eyes against them. She hated her own tears, her own emotion.

She hated that stupid, ticking clock.

She exploded from the chair, grabbed the clock, and lifted it over her head. But she couldn't throw it. Couldn't wreak any more destruction to things that mattered, not today.

Slowly she lowered the clock, turned it over, and removed the small, square battery that powered it. The ticking stopped.

15

Esperanza spent the next week trying to ignore the ache inside her by throwing herself into her work.

Most days and every evening, customers and potential customers came over to look at baby birds. Four times a day she mixed and heated formula to hand-feed a new clutch of cockatiels and one tiny Senegal parrot that was just starting to get its pin feathers.

Whatever free time she had she devoted to Paco, who was slowly but surely bonding to her. By using a system of rewards and gentle behavior modification, she had taught him to step up to a stick or her arm, to lie on his back and play dead, and to wave goodbye with one foot.

She tried to ignore Gabe, but it wasn't easy.

It wasn't that he tried to talk with her, to work things out, to explain or understand. On the contrary, he had stopped talking to her almost completely. Their few exchanges consisted of essential business; who would pick up groceries, or what time the plumber was arriving to fix the leak in the basement.

He wasn't coming home for dinner; in fact, he didn't come home until ten o'clock most evenings. Esperanza tried to harden herself to his absence and to avoid speculating about what he was doing, but it proved impossible. Could he have found another girlfriend this quickly? Was he spending the time with his family, building an ever-stronger case against her? Or was he just reverting to his old workaholic self?

He spent each night on the couch. In the morning she would find his blankets neatly folded, and Gabe himself already gone.

On the few evenings he came home earlier, though, his eyes followed her everywhere. Haunted, angry, or ice-cold. She started avoiding the rooms he was in.

When she came downstairs on Saturday morning, she expected to see him gone as usual, but he sat on the couch watching television. She paused at the doorway, but he didn't speak. Cowardly, she scuttled away into the kitchen and poured herself a cup of the coffee he'd made, then leaned against the counter looking at the pretty room she'd decorated.

She'd imagined this kitchen as a wonderful place for a family, with its multiple windows and space for a large table. Now, though, she and Gabe weren't even eating together. How long could they go on like this?

Suddenly she was gripped with loneliness so painful she almost bent double with it. She had to do something. Setting her coffee down, she walked toward the living room and stood in the doorway. "Gabe," she said quietly.

He didn't look at her; his eyes stayed fixed on the television. "Gabe!"

Turning slightly toward her, he raised his eyebrows. "Yes?" Then he looked back at the television and changed the channel.

Hurt and anger took her over then. She marched over to him, grabbed the remote control from his hand, and turned off the TV. "I can't live like this. Yell at me, throw things, do something, but don't just sit there judging me."

His face remained impassive. "This is how I am, Esperanza."

"What about how I am?"

He crossed his arms over his chest. "What would you rather do?" he asked, his voice cool. "Get into a knife fight?"

Gripping the edge of the TV stand, Esperanza stared at this man she loved. Visions of that long-ago night rushed back into her head: the fear, disgust, and horror; the self-loathing she'd spent years getting over. The room started spinning. Dimly she saw Gabe stand up.

"Are you all right?" he asked.

"I think I'm going to be sick," she said and ran for the powder room. She barely made it in time to slam the door behind her before she was violently ill, retching up the coffee that was all she had in her stomach.

When it was over, when she could stand up without shaking, she washed her face, rinsed her mouth, and looked at herself in the mirror. And in that moment of seeing her flushed, haunted face, she accepted the reality she'd been avoiding all week.

"It's just you again, kid," she told her reflection. The old lines came back from the countless times she'd done this as a child. "Time to move on. You'll be okay." Then her face crumpled and she buried it in her hands. It had been a long time, and a lot of moves, since she'd gotten so attached to a home. She should never have let it happen.

She had to get a grip on herself. She loved him, but that wasn't enough.

Because he didn't love her.

Oh, he might not know how much his words would hurt her. He definitely didn't know what the memory of that knife fight—the only one she'd ever been in—evoked in her mind.

But that was just it: he didn't know. And he didn't want to know. He wanted to stay in his clean, upper class world where people kept their problems under wraps and maybe took a lot of pills so they wouldn't have to deal with their own anger.

She knew she should pray now, and tried to. But she felt too sick to focus her mind on God.

She took some deep breaths and rinsed her face again.

"Esperanza. Are you okay?" It was Gabe's voice right outside the bathroom.

What did he care? And yet of course he didn't want her to get terribly ill or die or something, not on his watch.

She dried her face and opened the door. "I'm fine," she said, keeping her head down as she brushed past him and went upstairs.

As she looked around the bird room, her heart sank. There would be so much to move. Another change of address—this one moving downscale—might very well be the death of her business. "You don't want to move again, do you, Buster?" she asked, scratching the Amazon's green head through the bars of his cage.

Paco called a greeting to her and she moved to his cage and took him out. He seemed to sense her mood and snuggled against her, his large beak precise as he preened her hair. But even his comfort had a downside as he landed a macaw-sized dropping on her arm.

"Oh, Paco, yuck!" she said, and placed him on his T-stand.

"Paco, yuck!" he responded in a happy voice.

"Esperanza," Gabe said quietly from the door.

In the midst of grabbing a paper towel she turned toward him. "What?" She wiped at the mess on her sweater.

"You're right. We do need to talk."

Oh, so now he decided to communicate. "Look," she said. "It'll take me a couple of weeks to find a place to live where I can keep the birds. You'll have to put up with us—" she waved her hand around the bird room "—until April, but then we'll be out of your hair." She sidled past him and into the bedroom to change her sweater, carefully shutting the door behind her.

She'd thrown the dirty turtleneck into the hamper and was turning toward the bureau to pull out another shirt when the bedroom door opened.

Both of them froze.

Esperanza grabbed for the nearest sweatshirt and fumbled with it, finally finding the neck and sleeves and pulling it over her head. When she looked at Gabe again he stood in exactly the same place, staring at her.

She grabbed a brush and ran it quickly, angrily, over her mussed hair. Why had he violated the privacy of a closed door? Why now? And how much had he seen?

"What was that on your waist?" he asked.

"Nothing."

"It wasn't nothing," he said quietly. "It looked like a terrible scar."

Slamming the brush down on her dressing table, she turned to him. "That's right. It's a terrible, terrible scar. Any more questions?"

He walked a few steps toward her. "I . . . didn't see it before. The other night." His eyes flicked over her body.

Remembering that night, that sweet time before all of this history had slammed down on them, twisted at her heart. She set her jaw. "I kept my nightgown on, if you remember. And the light off."

"Was that why?" he asked. "I thought you were just being modest."

His voice was starting to go gentle. His eyes had softened. And Gabe being nice was the one thing she knew she couldn't tolerate. Opening to him again only meant more pain, and she'd reached her limit.

"A street fighter like me isn't modest," she said, deliberately putting a swagger in her voice. "I just didn't want you to start asking a lot of questions."

"So," he asked, "was even your modesty an act?" He walked closer until he was standing right in front of her, invading her space. His distinctive aftershave tickled her nose.

Hardening herself against the memories that smell evoked, she looked at him defiantly. "That's right. I'm surprised you didn't see through it. But then, you've always been a little naïve." She patted his cheek.

Gabe gripped her hand. His other arm came roughly around her shoulders and pulled her toward him. He started to say something, to scold, and Esperanza caught a wild glimpse of the man who'd raised his brother and sisters, who had been stern, a disciplinarian.

But then his face changed, the authority figure giving way to the hurt, frustrated lover. He tipped back her chin and kissed her hard, his tongue invading, his hand tangling in her hair, imprisoning her.

There was none of the gentleness he'd always shown her before. Rough, raw passion replaced it, a potent mix of fury and desire. Even in the midst of his anger, though, Gabe's lips were skilled, his tongue deft.

She broke away for a moment, gasping, but he took her mouth again. He was relentless, but not cruel. His tongue set up a rhythm, plunging, plundering. One hand came down to her hips and he slammed her against him.

It had to stop. To allow this heat to build any further would be insanity. But after the week of cold silence she'd endured, and with the loss and solitude that loomed before her, she couldn't break away. He'd said that physical fighting wasn't his style, but this loving felt like a fight. And she needed both: the fighting and the loving. She stood on tiptoe and put her arms around his neck, pulling him closer.

He moved her over to the bed and pushed her back down onto it, catching his weight with his arms as he fell atop her.

Her fears started swirling up then, but vaguely, masked by the pleasure his lips and tongue and teeth created. She felt things she'd never felt before. She hardly recognized the gasp of pleasure that came from her own mouth.

A moment later he pushed himself up to a sitting position, his hand going to his belt buckle.

So this was how she was going to lose her virginity.

To an angry man. One she loved with her whole heart.

One she was about to leave. She bit her lip, her heart pounding.

Gabe ran one finger over the angry red scar that curled down her side like a snake, twisting across her lower abdomen, disappearing under the waistband of her jeans. She flinched, and for the first time since he'd started kissing her, she pushed his hand away.

He caught her hand in his. "What's it from, Eppie?" His voice was hoarse.

"I don't want to talk about it."

"Tell me."

She drew in a deep breath and sighed it all out. Her desire escaped with her breath and dissipated into the bright morning sun that slanted into the bedroom. "That knife fight. With Wayne."

"I thought the knife was yours."

"It was. But he was bigger and stronger, and he turned it on me. And I'd rather not talk about it."

He reached toward the scar again, and again she shoved his hand away, then pulled her sweatshirt down.

Gripping the waist of her jeans, he propped himself on one elbow. "Okay, I won't ask any more questions about that. But there's something else I have to know."

"What?" She felt suddenly wary, on guard.

His voice was still thick with desire, and for once the careful

Gabe wasn't choosing his words carefully. "You're obviously not shy and modest, like I thought," he said. "Were you lying about being a virgin too?"

Esperanza clawed his hand away from her body and then scooted away from him on the bed, landing in a crouch at the headboard. "Get out of here."

"Why?" he asked, genuine surprise in his voice. "Maybe my style has been wrong all along, too slow, too careful—"

"Just get out." Her voice trembled and she gripped the headboard so hard that tears came to her eyes, but she wouldn't give him the satisfaction of seeing her cry.

He looked at her for a long time. It seemed to *take* a long time before he realized she meant what she said. Finally he stood and turned away from her to straighten his clothes. "I came in here," he said slowly, without looking at her, "to talk to you about splitting up. Right now I don't know what to think."

"I think," she whispered, "you were on the right track before."

He turned to face her, and when their eyes met there was such sadness in his that she had to lock her hands together to keep from reaching out to him.

"We could have been good together," he said. "You know that? If we could have stopped hurting each other, we could have been good."

The sound of the doorbell pierced the emotion-laden air.

"You'd better get that," she said, almost choking on the words. "I can't."

∽

WHEN HE SAW his mother standing in their entryway but looking back out the door, he thought something was wrong. Maybe it was the fact that her usually impeccable hair was messy.

"Mom!" he said, running his hands through his own mussed hair and hoping his face wasn't too flushed from the last half hour. Esperanza. How could one woman arouse such conflicting feelings in him, over and over and over?

"Gabriel," his mother said in an odd, quivery voice, "that awful bird has escaped."

"What bird?" He sprinted to the door to peer out beside her.

"That big red one. I'm not sure what happened."

His heart plunged as he saw a flash of red across the street. "Eppie!" he shouted. "Get down here!"

He ran out the door and toward the bird. Paco's wings were trimmed, but not as completely as some of the other birds because of his problem with feather-chewing. Even though Gabe slowed down as he got closer, Paco lifted his immense wings, caught a gust of wind, and flew halfway across the neighbor's lawn into a bush.

The wretched bird would never come to him. And there was no sign of Esperanza, which made sense considering the state he'd left her in. Why should she respond to his summons? He sprinted back to this house. "Watch that bird," he told his mother, nearly shoving her out the door, ignoring her whining complaints.

He took the stairs three at a time and burst into the bedroom. Esperanza was curled into a ball at the headboard where she'd been when he left, and she didn't lift her head.

"Eppie!" he said. "Paco escaped. You've got to come get him before he flies halfway across the county."

She did look up then, and stared at him blankly.

"I don't know how it happened," he said. "I guess he climbed down off his stand and went downstairs. When Mom opened the door, he must have flown out. Come on."

"Flew out... oh, no. It's too cold for him."

He nodded. "Hurry. He won't come to anyone but you."

She flew past him and out the bedroom door, and he heard her bare feet pattering down the stairs. "Get me some peanuts from the bird room," she yelled back at Gabe.

He grabbed a pair of her loafers and socks, and then a big bucket of peanuts, and ran after her.

Esperanza was shouting something at his mother, who was gesturing vaguely toward the end of the street.

She ran in that direction, her dark hair streaming out behind her. He caught her just as she stopped beneath a maple tree. High in its bare branches was Paco.

"Come on down, boy," she crooned, grabbing the peanut Gabe held out to her and extending it toward Paco. "Come on down. I can't lose you, too."

I can't lose you, too. Her words, which she probably hadn't even been aware of saying, suddenly brought home to Gabe what Esperanza had been suffering in the past week.

She'd lost her chance to adopt a baby.

She'd probably lost her husband and her home.

And now, she was in danger of losing one of the only beings who loved her unconditionally, without all of the judgement and arrogance of the human family.

The big bird cocked his head to one side, looking down at them with one eye. Then it started laughing, a chilling, human-sounding laugh.

"Boost me up there," Esperanza ordered Gabe.

"Put these on first." He held out her shoes.

"I can climb better barefoot. Boost me up."

He did as she asked, and she climbed toward Paco. When she was a couple of yards away, the bird lifted its magnificent wings and soared, landing in the middle of a lawn three houses down.

She shimmied down, her hands and feet scraped raw.

"Here," Gabe handed her the shoes. "Put these on. Easier to run."

A couple of neighbors had come out to watch the chase. Down the street a car pulled up in front of Gabe's and Esperanza's house and stopped. He saw Tanisha emerge and skip up toward the front door just as Esperanza finished shoving her feet into the loafers and ran toward the bird.

Gabe remembered that Tanisha had been helping Esperanza with the birds on Saturdays. Maybe Tanisha could help Esperanza. He jogged down the street toward the child, calling her name.

"Paco got out," he said as he reached her. "He likes you. Maybe you can help Esperanza corner him."

"Sure!"

He swung the girl up onto his shoulders—there were some benefits to being built like a lineman—and jogged after Esperanza.

When they were almost there, he stopped and lifted Tanisha to the ground, then filled her hands with peanuts. "Go around to the other side of the lawn," he said quietly.

Tanisha crept around and started closing in on the bird from the other side. Esperanza crouched and eased forward, holding out a peanut. "Come on, boy. Mom has a treat for you."

The bird watched her, interest and mischief in his face. When she got close, he started sidestepping away—straight toward Tanisha.

"Hold out your arm, Tanisha," Esperanza said quietly, still creeping toward the bird. "Just like we do in the bird room."

Tanisha extended a skinny brown arm, and Gabe looked at it doubtfully. Paco's beak could probably snap it in two.

"Tell him to step up."

"Step up," Tanisha said clearly as Paco reached her, pressing her arm against the bird's red chest.

Amazingly, the bird stepped up on the child's arm.

"Good boy!" Tanisha said, and handed Paco a peanut, which he grabbed with his foot and began to eat.

Esperanza approached and stuck out her own arm, gave a quiet command, and the bird obediently stepped onto her arm. She handed him another peanut.

"Be a baby," she ordered, cradling her arm.

Paco flipped over onto his back and lay in her arms.

"Tanisha, a peanut!" Eppie hissed, and the girl stood quickly and handed one to the bird.

The five or six neighbors who had emerged from their houses to watch the chase burst into applause as Esperanza stood and headed back toward their house, cradling the big red bird as if he were a baby. Tanisha walked proudly beside her, one hand reaching out occasionally to brush the red tail feathers.

When they got inside the house and closed the door, Esperanza sank down onto the bench in the front entryway. "Paco," she scolded, swinging the bird upright again. "You were a bad, bad boy."

"Bad boy," Paco agreed.

She snuggled him against her chest and scratched the feathers around his head. Gabe remembered the skinny, snarling creature the bird had been six months ago and marveled at the change that love and a good home had wrought.

"I guess you'd better enjoy that bird," Gabe's mother said, emerging from the living room. "It looks like that's the only baby you're going to get."

"Mom," Gabe warned.

"What's she mean, Miss Eppie?" Tanisha asked.

Esperanza looked at Gabe's mother carefully. Then she stood. "Come on, Tanisha, let's put this big guy back in his cage. And then we've got some hungry chicks to feed."

His mother's lip curled. "Rats with feathers."

"Why are you being like that, Mom?" Gabe asked, suddenly unable to put up with his mother's rude comments for another moment.

"Because she's stoned," Esperanza threw over her shoulder as she went up the stairs. "And by the way, I wouldn't let her drive home if I were you."

There it was again, Gabe thought in exasperation, the false allegation that had started all their problems. Sure enough, it got his mother going again. She uttered the ugliest phrase he'd ever heard from her cultured lips, staggered backward, and sat down hard on the bench Esperanza had just vacated.

"Mom. Try to be a little more careful about what you say to Esperanza."

"Don't you turn on me," she snapped at Gabe. "That young woman runs with the wrong crowd, and nothing that happens to her will surprise me."

He sat down next to his mother. "What crowd?"

"Oh, just her past, that's all. It's likely to catch up with her. Already started to." She looked at her watch. "My goodness. It's gotten to be lunchtime, and I'm due at the club." She stood, gripping the wall, and then walked toward the door.

"Mom, do you want me to drive you?" Even as he said it, Gabe frowned. What had made him ask that?

She spun, grabbed the door jamb, and glared at him. "I am perfectly capable of driving myself, no matter what that little hussy of yours says."

"Sure you are," he said quickly.

Still, he felt uneasy as he watched her pick her way down the driveway and climb into her Cadillac. When the engine started up he heard footsteps upstairs. Then Esperanza appeared, leaning over the banister.

"Don't let her drive, Gabe," she warned.

"She's fine!"

"She's not fine. And if you let her go and she has a wreck, her blood will be on your hands."

Gabe froze. For a moment he was at the scene of Melissa's death again, trying to cradle both her and their child as their life-blood drained away. Over his hands. Forever staining them.

He couldn't fix everything, couldn't control everything. That was becoming more apparent to him every day. But this, he could fix.

He ran coatless across the lawn toward his mother's car and yanked open the drivers' side door.

16

Two hours later, after taking his mother home, Gabe sat in Saint Joseph's Cathedral, feeling too low to go to confession as he'd intended.

The place evoked memories of his father, and that brought a tight throat and sense of shame. As the oldest son, Gabe had promised to protect and take care of the family. And yes, he's protected them, but he hadn't been a true leader morally.

And his family was falling apart.

He was starting to think Esperanza might be right about his mother. She had resisted his driving her, but in the end she'd agreed. And she'd also agreed to being taken home, rather than to the club where she'd been planning to have lunch. Once they'd arrived there, she'd staggered up to bed without saying more than a few slurred words to him.

He didn't think it was drinking, because he hadn't smelled any alcohol on her and he knew she hated the stuff. But there was definitely something wrong with her. Maybe she *was* going overboard with the pain pills.

If Esperanza was right, then he had been a fool. A narrow-minded, judgmental fool who couldn't see what was right in front of his eyes. An idiot who had taken the side of the mother he had always protected, instead of the wife who truly needed and deserved his support.

He got up, walked outside the church, and punched in Bianca's number.

"Do you have a minute?" And he told her his suspicions.

"I don't know," Bianca said doubtfully. "I mean, Mom's so straitlaced. It's hard to think of her as a drug addict."

"But a prescription drug addict is different," Gabe said. "It's not like she'd buy drugs out on the street, but if she got them from a doctor..."

"Would a doctor give her enough to get her addicted?"

"That's true. It's just... have you noticed how much worse she's gotten lately? The things she says?"

"No impulse control," Bianca said, and Gabe could tell that her psychology major background was kicking in. "You do have a point there."

"And slurred speech. And today, she was definitely staggering."

"Maybe," Bianca said slowly, "we should confront her about it. Do an intervention."

"Be direct? With Mom?"

"Maybe it's time we stopped coddling her," Bianca said. "Look, Nicki won't agree, but I'll talk to John. If he's noticed anything, I'll see if there's a day soon when we could just sit her down and talk to her."

"All right."

He was about to hang up when Bianca spoke again. "What are you going to do about Esperanza?"

"What do you mean?" Gabe stalled, though he thought he knew what she meant.

"You as much as told her she was lying about this," Bianca said slowly. "We all did. In fact, I wondered..."

"What?"

"I wondered if you were going to.... um... leave her."

He didn't want to deal with Bianca's questions. "I can't talk now."

"Okay," Bianca said. "Just don't wait too long to work it out with her, okay? Women can't take being hurt like that, not over and over again. Not even Esperanza."

Had he done that? Hurt her over and over again?

And then he thought of her crouched by the headboard of their bed, her lips still swollen with his kisses, after he'd accused her of lying about her virginity. He thought of the hurt in her eyes.

Yet she had warned him not to let his mother drive. Even in her pain, in what was almost certainly anger or even hatred of him, she had thought beyond herself to the safety of a woman who despised her.

Whatever her flaws, she had a generosity of spirit that took his breath away.

"I'll talk to you later, Bianca," Gabe said quickly and clicked off the call. Then he sat on the cathedral steps, head in hands, while his thoughts whirled.

Bianca had accepted the idea of their mother's possible addiction with far less shock than he'd thought. Maybe Esperanza had been right all along.

Maybe she'd been right about more than one thing.

She had deceived him about her past, letting him think she was just a victim, when it turned out that she'd actually been arrested and put into a juvenile detention center. Although the charges had eventually been dropped, the revelation made unlikely that they'd be picked by birth mothers to adopt.

Even so, when he thought of the angry red scar on her torso, he felt ashamed that he hadn't waited to hear the whole story before condemning her. He had gotten swept away with the surprise of it, and with Nicola's vindictive attitude, and had listened to her slant on the story.

But he well knew there were two sides to every story. Nicola had heard it from Wayne, the man Esperanza had attacked; of course he would take a different perspective than would Eppie.

The vibration of his phone jarred him out of his thoughts. When he answered the unfamiliar number, Rhonda's voice on the other end of the line subjected him to every colorful expletive in the name-calling book.

After a couple of sputtering efforts he succeeded in breaking into her tirade. "Hey. Do you mind slowing down and telling me *why* I'm worse than pond scum?"

"Because," Rhonda said, "I just ran into your snotty little sister, and she told me the adoption plan is off and you and Eppie have broken up over something she heard from Wayne the Psycho. Are you out of your mind?"

"Your information's a little exaggerated," he said. "We haven't broken up. It's true I'm upset about what I learned about Esperanza's past, but that's between the two of us."

"It sounds like your family and Wayne are involved too," Rhonda said. "And if that's the case, then I can just guess how everything's gotten twisted around, because Wayne hates Eppie and me both, and your family isn't so thrilled about us either. And I'm coming over to that adoption agency first thing Monday morning to set the record straight."

"Uh, okay," Gabe said. "I'd be glad to hear your point of view."

"I don't give a hang about you," Rhonda said. "But it's not right that Eppie is going to lose her chance at adopting a baby because of that jerk. He already took away her chance of having a baby of her own, and—"

"He did what?"

"That knife fight and the scarring. It was so like her, not to tell anyone how bad she was hurt, until she practically died from the infection. The doctors told her she might not ever be able to have kids. You . . . did know about all that, right?"

Gabe couldn't speak.

"Okay, maybe you don't know. In fact, I'm wondering if you know anything at all about your wife."

Gabe let his forehead sink into his hand. Eppie couldn't have children? Because of this knife fight? And she'd never told him?

Rhonda's voice, ridden with sudden anxiety, broke through the silence. "Hey, tell me something. Where is Eppie right now?"

"At home," he said.

"No, she's not. I called over there and there was no answer."

"I don't know where she would have gone. When I left a couple of hours ago, she and Tanisha were taking care of the birds."

"Oh, well, maybe she took Tanisha home," Rhonda said. "I just all of a sudden got a little freaked because there was a crank message on my machine last night. You know, a breather? You been getting those?"

"A couple of hang-ups," he said slowly.

"But Nicola wouldn't have told Wayne where we live, would she?"

"I think she did. Why?"

"Because," she said, speaking as if he were extremely slow, "Wayne hates Esperanza. Well, he hates me too, but especially her. He's tried to find her for a long time. That's why she left the city, and that's why she's scared to advertise there about her birds. He's stalked her before."

"Stalked—" Gabe stood and headed for his car. "Rhonda, I'm going home to make sure she's okay."

"I'll meet you there," Rhonda said promptly.

"Don't—"

But Rhonda had already hung up.

When she heard the car door slam in front of the house, Esperanza felt a wave of emotion wash over her.

Gabe had come back. Thank the Lord. Despite all that had happened, she loved him.

Oh, his questioning of her honesty twisted a knife in her heart. But who could blame him when he had just discovered a whole dark past he'd not known she had?

His family was difficult. Never again would she pray for a family, any family. She had realized through Gabe that having a family didn't guarantee emotional health and happiness. But his family wasn't his fault, it was his burden.

Esperanza wanted to help him carry his burdens. In the midst of their worst fight ever he had dropped his negative feelings about her to help her save Paco. They were a team. They could pull together.

But would he be willing to try?

Hearing the front door open, Esperanza hung back in the bird room, wanting a little more time to prepare herself mentally.

If he came back, if he agreed to try it again, she knew they had to be together as husband and wife. She couldn't keep to herself any longer, couldn't postpone the moment of truth. And she wondered, now, if she really wanted to. Since he had seen her scars, one of the worst aspects of intimacy was already past.

And earlier today, her hunger for closeness had almost matched his. It was definitely time.

Taking a deep breath, mentally preparing herself to fight for a relationship that she was only now starting to believe *might* have a chance, Esperanza walked down the stairs.

"Gabe?" she called softly, leaning into the kitchen and looking around.

Hearing his footstep behind her, she turned.

And saw Wayne.

Esperanza's heart jumped and then settled into a huge, heavy pounding that almost blocked the sound of his sinister laugh. Her fingernails dug into the door jamb.

"Scared you, did I?"

"How did you get in here?" She barely recognized the low, tight voice as her own.

Wayne's smile wasn't a smile, not really. "You made it easy. I just walked in the front door. It was like you were waiting for me."

"I was waiting," she said, "for my husband. He's coming home any minute."

"I don't think so," Wayne said, cracking his knuckles.

A wave of disgust passed over Esperanza as the familiar gesture brought back the old days and weeks of intimidation, threats, and then the horrible reality behind the threats. She had learned the hard way that Wayne meant every nasty innuendo that he said. "What do you mean," she asked, feeling like she couldn't breathe, "you don't think so?"

Wayne walked toward her slowly, and just as slowly, never taking her eyes off him, she backed into the kitchen. When she felt the kitchen counter behind her she stopped. Wayne's slight smile told her how much he enjoyed literally backing her into a corner. "I happened to follow him to the cathedral. Unfortunately, your husband had a couple of flat tires. On a busy Saturday, it'll take awhile for him to fix them."

"You didn't."

"What?" Wayne's voice held a fake innocence. Then he broke the illusion with a nasty smile. "Okay, I did it. I just wanted us to have a talk. For old time's sake. You're practically my sister, and we haven't seen each other for, what, six years?"

"Eight years. I was seventeen."

"And so was I." Wayne continued smiling as he moved a few inches closer. "We're just the same age. That husband of yours is an old man. Comes from a stuck-up family, too." His mouth twisted a little to one side, and Esperanza's stomach clenched. She remembered that expression. He was getting angry. "You should have heard them talking to me like I was stupid. Looking at me like I was something you'd scrape off the bottom of your shoe. Oh, but they were glad enough to find me and get the dirt on you. I gave it to 'em good, too."

Esperanza crossed her arms across her midsection and tried to think. *Delay, delay,* some survivalist voice shouted in her mind. She had no doubt of Wayne's intentions. He meant to hurt her, maybe even kill her, after he was finished with whatever twisted torture would ease his sense of vengeance.

Her only chance was to keep him talking until somebody came, or until she could see a free path to a door. In a physical contest, she had little chance. Wayne wasn't tall, but he was stocky, his long arms muscular, his legs thick and stumpy. Built like an animal, Rhonda had always said.

Some of the contempt she felt must have shown on her face, because Wayne moved closer still, his voice low and threatening. "You're looking at me that way too. Think you're better than me now, do you?" He laughed in her face and she smelled his stale breath and the faint-but-pungent odor of his body. A rush of memories overwhelmed her and she half-turned away.

"You ain't nothing but gutter trash yourself, and don't you forget it," he snarled, and then he slapped her, hard.

Esperanza doubled over, her hands flying up to protect herself. In a flash she saw how far she'd come since her teenage years, because this physical assault so shocked her. Back then, she would have expected it. She looked up and tried to see around Wayne to the window, hoping without real hope that Gabe or someone would show up.

"Your old man ain't stickin' by you," Wayne said. "He's not your kind. Forget about him. You may as well go back to where you belong." He paused, then smiled. "To your family."

"You're not my family."

"I'm what you've got."

She straightened up cautiously. Her mind went into overdrive, thinking of how to slow him down. "You're right," she said, hating the words. She'd used to be a better liar. "I guess you are my family, in a way." She hazarded an effort at distraction. "You and Rhonda."

He called Rhonda a name that made Esperanza boil inside.

But she couldn't let him see that. "Have you seen her?"

He laughed and sneered at the same time, something she'd never seen anyone but Wayne accomplish. "Yeah, I saw her. Knocked up, ain't she?"

Esperanza nodded. "She's going to the Free Clinic. Where you work."

"I know. I saw you that day."

"You did?"

Wayne nodded. "Uh-huh. I couldn't follow you, or I might have lost my job. But you know, that was a funny thing. Right after I saw the two of you in there, they started watching me closer. Didn't let me near the patients. Asked me a lot of questions." He reached out and caught her upper arm in a grip that got slowly tighter. "You wouldn't happen to know anything about that, would you?"

"No."

"Liar!" He jerked her arm and she felt like it was coming out of the socket. "I'm friends with a gal there. She told me they got a phone call. Some woman, making all kinds of warnings. All the girls were talking about it."

She saw now that he had been holding himself back, that his

rage was personal and of recent vintage. For a moment her mind went blank with fear.

But that was what had happened years ago. She'd gotten too scared, and her mind had stopped working, and the results had stayed with her to this day. She couldn't let that happen again. She had to think.

"Wayne, it wasn't me who called," she lied desperately. "I would never do that to you."

He twisted her arm behind her, moving closer, and she fought the revulsion she felt. "I *said*, don't lie to me! I know you've always hated me for what I did."

"The past is the past. Why would I bring it up again? I hoped ... I hope ... you've gotten over all of that."

Studying her, he said, "Then it must have been Rhonda who called."

"No! It wasn't her."

"How do you know it wasn't her—unless it was you?" he said with a nasty laugh. "You are so easy, girl. You'd never let me think it was Rhonda. You'd always try to protect her. Just like back then."

So that ruse hadn't worked. "You always did know me pretty well," she said, once again trying for delay. "But how did you find me, anyway?"

He grinned. "You made it easy for me when you changed your name. There are about a million people named 'Acosta' in the city, but only a few Montanas out here in Hopewell Corners. Once your lovin' in-laws came to see me, it was pretty simple to find you."

"Oh," she nodded. "Um, what have you been doing, anyway?"

He pushed her back against the counter, hard. "This *ain't* a social call, sister. I came here 'cause I have business with you."

"Oh, really?" she said, trying not to retch at his nearness. "And what would that be?"

He pressed against her. "I'm gonna finish what I started years ago. And I think you know just what I mean."

Hearing him say the words made her frantic. In a rush she discarded the idea of talking him out of it. Someone like Wayne wouldn't listen to talk. With her free arm she jerked up and took a swift jab at his eyes, at the same time lifting her knee as hard as she could.

"Ugggh!" Wayne didn't seem to know where to grab as he doubled over. Esperanza took advantage of this momentary weakness to kick him as hard as she could, throwing him off balance. On the way out of the kitchen she slowed down just enough to throw the toaster at him for good measure, and she felt an instant of streetfighter's satisfaction as it connected with the side of his face.

But she still had her streetfighter's sense of timing, too, and it told her she had about one minute, maximum, before he regrouped and came back at her madder than ever. Her assault had taken him by surprise, but she just wasn't strong enough to disable him.

In the entryway she ran head-on into Rhonda.

"What the--hey . . . slow down, girl," Rhonda said, catching her forearms.

"We gotta run! Wayne's here!"

Rhonda didn't need to be told twice. She spun around and yanked open the front door.

"Freeze. Or I'll shoot the both of you."

Something about Wayne's deadly tone made them both go still. In slow motion they turned around.

Wayne stood at the other end of the hall, a big, mean-looking gun aimed straight at them.

Esperanza swallowed the bile that rushed into her throat.

Beside her she heard Rhonda's whispered curse. She stepped in front of her foster sister. "Get out," she said to Rhonda. "Now. It's me he's after anyway."

Wayne strolled slowly toward them. "Hang on, Rhonda. I got a bone to pick with you too."

"She didn't make that phone call, Wayne. She didn't even want me to. It was my idea, and she tried to talk me out of it."

He shook his head, a twisted smile on his face. "You haven't changed a lick, have you? Always trying to protect the others, even the trash like this one."

"Let her go, Wayne. She's pregnant, for heaven's sake. You don't want that on your conscience."

Oddly, that seemed to infuriate him more. "She didn't keep *my* baby," he snarled.

Esperanza's hand flew to her mouth. She stepped away from Rhonda and stared at her, then at Wayne. "You didn't. When?"

"Remember those months you were in the detention center?" He laughed again. "Surprised?"

"Oh, honey," Esperanza said helplessly to Rhonda, tears welling up in her eyes. "I'm so sorry. You should have told me!"

Rhonda's eyes were fixed on Wayne. "Get over it, Eppie. I did."

"Yeah, fast as you could, you cold witch."

"Believe it or not, I miscarried that baby," Rhonda said with no expression in her voice. "I'm told it happens pretty often to girls who get pregnant that young."

Wayne strolled slowly toward them. "You lie."

"Why would I bother? You're not worth lying to."

"I'm glad you walked in here, Rhonda. Saves me the trouble of huntin' you down."

His attention was off her, and Esperanza took advantage of that moment, and her fury, to grab a statue from the hall table. She knew she had only one chance.

She raised it high over her head.

Just as she started to bring it down he seemed to see her from the corner of his eye. He swung around, and as the gun came to point at her, Esperanza's heart seemed to stop beating.

She was going to die.

And she had never had a chance to tell Gabe what it meant to her that he'd taken a chance, that he'd tried to make a go of it with her.

Help me, Lord.

And then it all happened at once.

The statue came down on Wayne's shoulder, not his head as she'd planned, but it was enough to make his shot go wild. Esperanza dove to the ground. Almost instantly, there was another shot, and Wayne got the oddest look of surprise on his face as his legs went out from under him.

"Huh," Rhonda said, staring down at the small, silver-plated gun in her hand. "This old thing really works." Her eyes were glassy with shock.

Esperanza tried to speak, to ask where Rhonda had gotten a gun. But then she saw, from where she lay on the hall floor, that Wayne's hand was still wrapped around his own gun. He raised it and pointed it at Rhonda.

She screamed at the top of her lungs.

Wayne turned the gun on her.

And then there was something dark and heavy and enormous flying through the air. It landed half on her, half on Wayne. Esperanza heard the sickening sound of a bone breaking and another gunshot.

Only then could she lift her head, dazed, to understand that it was Gabe who had landed on her and on Wayne.

She pushed herself out from under Wayne with a strength she'd never felt before. Had Wayne's shot found a target in the man she loved?

Slowly Gabe pushed himself up from the floor. He extricated Wayne's gun from what looked to be a very broken arm and studied Wayne's gray, sagging face. "He's out," Gabe said, and then looked at her. "Are you hit? Are you all right?"

"I'm fine," she said quickly. "Rhonda?"

They both turned to see Rhonda sinking down onto the bench beside the front door. "And to think my doctor told me not to overexert myself," she said. "This is too much for a pregnant lady."

"You're okay?" Esperanza asked anxiously.

"I'm fine. I guess. For just having shot someone." She leaned over and studied Wayne as he lay, apparently unconscious, on the floor. The expression on her face was one of extreme distaste. "That was something I've wanted to do for a real long time."

"Me too, sister." Esperanza gave Rhonda a fist-bump and then a huge hug.

17

Hours later, when the doorbell wouldn't stop ringing, someone finally opened it.

A small, dark-haired fireball came in. "Am I too late?"

Esperanza, who'd been flopped on the couch like a rag doll, opened her eyes. That voice was familiar. "Maria?"

"Eppie!" The woman ran to her, knelt in front of her. Esperanza tried to sit up, to lean forward, but her body refused to agree. "Where is he? What did he do to you? I came as soon as Rhonda called me—"

Rhonda came in from the kitchen. "Girl, you missed all the action. I shot Wayne, but didn't kill him, unfortunately. He's in custody. But I have a social worker and a cop who'd like to talk to you."

Maria hugged Esperanza, then leaned back and looked at her seriously. "I'll tell all about what happened when we were kids."

"Will you tell Gabe, too?"

Maria glanced over at Rhonda.

"They haven't been believing me," Rhonda said grimly. "But together, we'll set them straight."

Everyone except Esperanza trooped into the kitchen. The conversations went on a long time, first with the detectives and a social worker, and then between Rhonda, Maria, and Gabe.

A couple of detectives spoke to Esperanza separately and offered a visit to the ER. She turned it down. Finally left in peace in the living room, she curled into a ball on the couch.

She wanted to sleep, but of course, her adrenaline was too high. She rested her cheek against the couch's velvety fabric and let her mind drift.

I am with you.

She didn't hear the words aloud, but they were clear as a spoken sentence in her mind and she knew their source.

I will never leave you or forsake you.

Father God had shown her that. Even in the worst moment with Wayne, he'd been there, strength in the storm.

We love because He loved us first. She hadn't felt loveable, not ever, not really. But now, in the dark room, His love surrounded her like a downy blanket.

Grief about Gabe lay heavy on her heart. But even going on alone, she felt a measure of peace. She was a child of God, and He loved her. That wouldn't go away, not ever.

Later, Maria insisted on taking Rhonda to the hospital to be checked out, much against her will. "You're pregnant and you shot a man. At least see a doctor, and then let me take you home and make you chicken soup," Maria scolded, practically dragging Rhonda out the door.

"You're all right?" Rhonda popped her head back in to ask Esperanza.

Esperanza nodded, touched to the core by Rhonda's protectiveness.

"Let her talk to her husband," Maria said sternly. "We'll see you tomorrow," she added to Esperanza.

The door shut behind them.

Now it was just she and Gabe. In their home. Which would probably not be *their* home much longer, but which still felt like a welcome relief after the most incredibly emotional day Esperanza had ever experienced.

And even with God's comfort and love clinging to her, she still felt on the verge of tears. Who wouldn't, after such a day? When she had thought of losing her life with all these misunderstandings remaining between Gabe and herself, the ache in her heart had swept away any last remnants of doubt: she loved him.

The ache had been almost as much for Gabe as for herself. She had thought of him losing another wife. Thought of his guardedness, his incredible control and strength that allowed him to hide his wounds from the rest of the world.

If she died, she would never have the chance to make up for betraying him, for lying to him, if not directly, then by omission. He would think she had not cared. He would think she had used him for what he could give her. And he would never know of her love for him, the love that swelled her heart.

She didn't want him ignorant any longer. No matter that their marriage was a sham. No matter that the past few hours had proven beyond any doubt that her background was too chaotic, too mired in dirt and crime and violence to meld comfortably to any normal family, any normal man. Even so, she wanted him to know of her regret at what they might have had if life had dealt them different cards.

And she wanted him to know her last great secret. "Gabe?" she called.

He walked into the room and stood before her. His face shadowed with stubble and weariness, he looked at her, and she was surprised to see the churning emotions there. Maybe he was too exhausted to maintain the curtain that usually veiled his deepest feelings.

She spoke before she could lose her courage. "I have something to tell you."

"Go ahead."

"I . . . When I got my scars, you know . . ." She cleared her throat and started again. "There was an infection."

He nodded.

"Gabe, it means I might not be able to have children," she blurted out in a rush. "I know I should have told you before. I thought it would be okay because we were just going to adopt, but then all these problems came up . . . well, there's no excuse. I married you under false pretenses. You had every right to know you were getting damaged goods." She hesitated, unable to look at him. "There's no reason we can't get an annulment. We haven't, you know, consummated the marriage. No one would fault you after all you've been through with me."

He stood still, an inscrutable expression on his face. The silence seemed to last for hours, broken only by the late-night music on the classical station in the kitchen.

"Do you want to talk?" she asked finally.

He looked at her for a moment more. "No," he said.

"Do you want me to leave now? I could maybe stay at Rhonda's, until—"

"No."

She was too worn out to try any longer. His short answers were tearing her apart, and she was afraid she'd make a fool of herself and start to cry outright. So she stared at the braided rug and listened to the grandfather clock they'd received as a wedding present, and waited.

At last Gabe cleared his throat. "I want to ask you a favor," he said, his voice as serious as she'd ever heard it.

"Okay." She was scared to look at him.

"I want you to come to bed with me tonight."

Her head shot up and she stared at him, trying to understand what she was hearing. "You mean..."

He nodded slowly, his eyes never leaving hers.

"But why? Why would you want to after... everything that's happened?"

He lifted his hands helplessly. "Because I can't find any words to say to you. I wonder if there's another language besides words. And don't want this marriage to end without really being a marriage."

"We couldn't... get an annulment then."

"I know."

Letting her head flop back against the couch, Esperanza studied him. He was too gentle to push her, but he had been put through more than almost any man would tolerate, being repeatedly deceived, and living together for this long without physical release. She had promised to be fully his wife. Now, he was cashing in on that promise.

She loved him, loved him more than she'd known was possible. And he was her lawful husband. "All right," she said.

"Are you sure?"

She nodded. It was the least she could do for him, if he really wanted it.

He held out a hand to her, and she was surprised to see that it was trembling. Had he been that afraid she would say no? Wonderingly she looked into his eyes.

When she saw the barely veiled desire her hand froze halfway to his. Her heart pounded, drumming out a song of fear and something else she barely recognized in herself.

"Are you sure?" he asked again.

"I'm sure."

He reached out and took her hand, pulled her up, and

crushed her against him. She wrapped her arms around him and turned her face to the side. Against his chest she could hear the steady thumping of his heart; beneath her cheek, she felt the scratchy wool of his sweater.

A trembling started deep inside her, but it was soothed by the feel of his gentle hands on her hair. And then he reached down and picked her up, cradling her against his chest, moving quickly up the stairs.

Much later, in the quiet of their bedroom, Gabe helped her ease herself to his side and tucked her into the curve of his massive shoulder.

"I'm sorry it hurt," he said. "That part will get better, with time."

Esperanza lost her breath. "Do we . . . have time?" she managed finally.

He propped himself on one elbow so he could see her, and she could have sworn the look on his face wasn't just lust, but love. But that didn't make any sense.

"You're not mad at me?" she asked.

"Did I seem mad, just now?"

She shook her head. "But my . . . infertility." It was still hard to say the word, even after all these years. "It doesn't make you disappointed in me?"

Shaking his head, he found with his finger the scar that snaked cross her midsection and stroked it. "I knew already," he admitted. "Rhonda told me, earlier today."

"Then why would you come back?"

"Just because you had something awful happen to you," he said, "does that mean I should condemn you? It's more to do with your pain than my needs."

His words swirled around her. He wasn't condemning her. He was sympathetic to what had happened to her, to her ordeal. "What are you saying?"

"Eppie," he said, stroking her arm, "I don't care if we can't have children together. We can probably work out some way to adopt. I just want to be with you. When I thought I might lose you today . . . " He shook his head and looked across the bedroom, then back into her eyes, and this time she could definitely read the love there. "I want you for you. Not for what you can give me. For you."

Something dissolved in Esperanza then. She couldn't remember ever in her life being loved without conditions, without demands, except by God.

Touching his broad shoulders, she looked into his eyes. "You know," she said, "I've always thought I had to adopt a baby, because a therapist told me I was too messed up to handle an older child and the problems they faced," she said. "Now, I'm thinking all of a sudden that that might not be true anymore."

"You do pretty well with Tanisha."

She nodded. "And, weird as it seems, with Paco."

Gabe laughed. "If you could turn that nasty beast into a big loving baby, a troubled child shouldn't be any problem at all."

"You wouldn't mind an older child?"

Shaking his head, Gabe stroked her face tenderly. "Together I think we could provide a wonderful home for a troubled kid. Or two. But I have to tell you, Rhonda plans to set the record straight about what really happened with Wayne. Maria, too. Once the agency knows the whole story, we'll fit the new guidelines I've been putting into place. I'm pretty confident that we'll be back on the baby list."

She knew everything she felt shone in her eyes, but she didn't care. For once, she had nothing to hide. No secrets. No hidden shame. "We can start having a real home together," she whispered.

"We can start right now." And he took her into his arms.

EPILOGUE

"Come in, everybody come in!" Tanisha's excited voice echoed through the house, and Esperanza clattered down the stairs to greet her friends.

It was Tanisha's ninth birthday.

Her *daughter* Tanisha's ninth birthday.

Even though it had been almost six months since Tanisha had come to live with them, Esperanza still felt a sense of wonder whenever she did one of those motherly things. Attending parent-teacher conferences, leading a Girl Scout Troop, or, like today, hosting a birthday party—she wondered if she would ever take any of it for granted. This adoption, which would be finalized within a matter of weeks, seemed like such a special blessing.

Oh, they had had their challenges. Tanisha and Gabe had taken some time to grow closer, and they had had to lay out clear rules and boundaries to help the child learn discipline. But now, watching Gabe try to balance at least six brightly-wrapped gifts in one arm while Tanisha clung to his other hand, Esperanza thought they looked like any other father and daughter.

Even more of a wonder was the fact that Gabe's mother was

among the family group that had entered the room. Gabe's mother, sober and drug-free.

The woman gave Esperanza a stiff little hug, and Esperanza greeted her warmly. They weren't the best of friends even now, but the progress they had made was impressive. Now that Mrs. Montana could control her impulses, she didn't say the hurtful things that had regularly come out of her mouth before, and since she wasn't constantly destroying her relationships, people were nicer to her. The cycle was turning upward.

Tanisha was excitedly studying her presents and examining the labels. "Can I open them?" she asked.

Gabe looked at Esperanza and shrugged. And this, too, Esperanza treasured. The parental love she felt as her eyes met her husband's, as they read each other's minds.

"We should wait until everyone gets here," Esperanza said. "But I think you can open one now."

"You choose," Gabe said to Tanisha.

"I'll open the one from Grandma," Tanisha said after a moment's thought. "It's the biggest." She ripped into the bright wrapping paper and shouted with delight at the enormous stuffed bear. Immediately she wrapped her arms around it.

"It's perfect," Esperanza murmured to Mrs. Montana. "She loves teddy bears better than any other toy." Esperanza knew that many nine-year-olds were beyond stuffed toys, but not Tanisha. The child had missed some of the earlier developmental stages in her life as a foster child, and now that she was safe in a permanent home, she was making up for lost time. According to Tanisha's social worker, it was a perfectly healthy development.

What was even more striking was that Mrs. Montana had sensed the perfect gift for Tanisha. In an odd way, her own pain and difficulty had sensitized her even as she struggled at times with the idea of a biracial grandchild.

Tanisha ran to Mrs. Montana and threw her arms around her, the giant bear between them, and even Mrs. Montana couldn't resist. She sank down to her knees and hugged the little girl.

Bianca put an arm around Esperanza. "I can't thank you enough for helping us figure out what was going on with Mom," she said. "She's better than she's ever been. I mean, a few months ago, would you have believed this scene?"

"Give Tanisha some of the credit," Esperanza said. "She's pretty hard to resist."

The doorbell started ringing steadily then. First it was the three friends Tanisha had invited from school, then Gabe's brother John.

Next, Maria and her husband, Hector, arrived with their son, Jaxon, a sturdy and energetic two-year-old. Esperanza had renewed her relationship with Maria since she'd helped give the police information about Wayne, and she'd visited Maria and Hector in Pittsburgh. So Esperanza, she of the small, almost nonexistent family, had another sister to love, more supportive family members to celebrate with on occasions like this.

Blessed. She was blessed.

Rhonda arrived next, her infant carrier in one hand, a giant diaper bag slung over her shoulder, and a bag from a local toy chain extended in front of her. "Eppie," she said, sounding harassed, "Hon, I didn't have time to wrap this. Do you think you could—"

"Sure, I'll get it wrapped." She peeked inside and then rolled her eyes at Rhonda. "A Barbie? With purple fingernails and blue hair?"

"It's not a Barbie, it's Rapper RayLean," said Rhonda. "Haven't you heard of her?"

"Rapper RayLean? You got me a Rapper RayLean?" Tanisha

cried ecstatically, and her three friends squealed and gathered around Rhonda and Esperanza.

Esperanza shook her head and handed the bag to the eager girls.

Rhonda grinned at her. "I know what you're thinking," she said, "but don't worry. She's a girl-power rapper. She doesn't curse, and she's all about respecting yourself."

"And her skirt is half-an-inch long," Esperanza said, laughing a little as she watched Tanisha rip open the doll's box. "Thanks, Rhonda."

"There's a link to download her music in there. Listen to it. You'll see."

"I don't think we have much choice," Esperanza said, watching Tanisha and her friends rush to borrow a cell phone. "Play it quietly, girls," she said. "We don't want to wake up the baby."

"He'll sleep through anything," Rhonda said, jiggling the carrier fondly. "I play my music loud all the time."

The doorbell rang again, and Esperanza's heart pounded as she greeted Sofia Sanchez. "Come on in and sit down, honey," she said to the very pregnant sixteen-year-old.

"*En Espanol,*" Sofia scolded as she waddled to the couch and sank down.

"Oh, sorry. *Lo siento,*" Esperanza said. "*Como estas?*"

"*Estoy bien, gracias,*" Sofia said and then switched to English. "You have to practice all the time, Eppie."

"I know, you're right. I've been studying and listening to the tapes, honestly. Even the birds are learning Spanish."

"Good," Sofia said, "because I want my baby to be bilingual."

"I want that too," Esperanza said softly.

Gabe quickly made his way over. "How are you feeling?" he asked Sofia anxiously. "Do you think the baby will come early?"

"I hope so," Sofia said. "I'm tired of being so big. I can't wait to fit into my clothes again."

Always attuned to references to fashion, Rhonda strolled over. "Don't hold your breath," she advised Sofia. "You don't get back your size six right away. Believe me, I know."

Immediately the two were enmeshed in a detailed conversation about abdominal exercises and styles that concealed extra weight. Gabe shrugged and leaned back, clearly out of his element.

Esperanza went to get birthday punch for everyone. She could hardly contain the joy in her heart.

A home. A husband. A large extended family.

A nine-year-old daughter *and* a baby on the way.

In the kitchen she paused and murmured a quick prayer of thanksgiving.

As she stood, her head bowed, she felt Gabe's arms encircle her from behind.

"Hey," he whispered. "What's going on?"

She turned in his arms to face him, smiling. "Just happy," she said.

"Me, too," he said. "I think we'd better put the finishing touches on the nursery pretty soon, don't you?"

"I can't wait."

"You know," Gabe said, "Tanisha asked if she could spend the night with Andrea. Think we could take advantage of having the house to ourselves tonight, before the baby comes?"

Esperanza met his eyes, saw the unmistakable desire there, and felt a slow burning inside. "So, how long before we can kick our guests out?"

"Give me ten minutes," Gabe said.

∽

THANK you for reading the Sacred Bond Guardians series! If you haven't read the earlier books, turn the page to find a complete listing.

∼

If you've completed this series, have you read the original Sacred Bond novels? These contemporary romances focus on the first group of boys from the Covenant School. **Grab the boxed set at a deep discount**, or pick up these individual titles:

A CHRISTMAS BOND (CHRISTIAN ROMANCE): Sacred Bond Series Prequel Novella

War hero John Moretti must work with crime victim Annie Bauer to restore the Baby Jesus to Annie's grandmother's yard nativity scene... or risk sending the boys he mentors straight to juvie.

HIS BABY BOND (CHRISTIAN ROMANCE): Sacred Bond Series Book 1

On a Colorado mountaintop, poor-but-proud Kendra Forrester battles millionaire Zeke King for custody of the baby they both love...

THE BRIDE'S Broken Bond (Christian Romance): Sacred Bond Series Book 2

Poor little rich girl Hope DeMille runs away from her high-society wedding, straight into the inner city...and into the brawny arms of urban missionary Rock Anderson.

. . .

Her Reunion Bond (Christian Romance): Sacred Bond Series Book 3

What if your high school boyfriend came back to town...and moved in next door?

The Doctor's Bond (Christian Romance): Sacred Bond Series Book 4

The bad boy from the wrong side of the tracks is now a respected doctor...but he's still a little too edgy for the proper preacher's daughter. Or is he?

THE COMPLETE SACRED BOND GUARDIANS SERIES...

Check out all the Sacred Bond Guardians novels:

The Protector's Bond, Prequel Novella, Chad and Lissa

A Brother's Bond, Book One, Adam and Karen

A Bond at Risk, Book Two, Travis and Amber

A Bond of Vengeance, Book Three, Jake and Kendra

A Bond Fulfilled, Book 4, Hector and Maria

A Western Bond, Book 5, Mark and Serena

A Bond of Hope, Book 6, Gabe and Esperanza

And visit Lee's website to learn about the original Sacred Bond series, as well as her latest bestselling books from Harlequin. Join her newsletter there as well... get a free novella just for signing up!

WHAT TO READ NEXT...

Wondering what to read next? I'd recommend my Safe Haven series of longer romances, published by HQN. Like the Sacred Bond Guardians, the Safe Haven series focuses on romance with a good dose of suspense.

Set in the South Carolina Low Country and centered on a community known for helping women in need, the Safe Haven series gives you the same sweet, wholesome reading experience as the Sacred Bond books... in a bigger way. Turn the page to sample *Low Country Hero*.

LOW COUNTRY HERO... SNEAK PEEK!

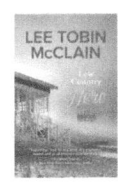

Prologue

October 15, 1996

Walking from the small-town grocery store back toward their new home at the Safe Haven women's shelter, Rita O'Dwyer felt her shoulders start to relax. Maybe this was going to be okay. For her boys, and even, maybe, for her.

They passed a little tourist stand, full of South Carolina beach trinkets and toys.

"Mom, can we go in?" her middle boy, Cash, pleaded. "Please?" He was the most materialistic of her three sons, and she always joked that he'd become a billionaire, but his strong focus worried her a little. Today, like any other kid, he just wanted to see the toys.

She paused. Even her oldest, Sean, leaned past his brothers to look in the little shop, and of course her baby, Liam, joined in the begging. "Please, Mommy? There's swords and stuff!"

They sounded like normal kids. Normal, wonderfully-whiney kids, and she couldn't resist their request.

She ached with the desire to give her boys a normal

childhood.

While the boys looked at the beachy souvenirs, Rita fingered a little five-dollar necklace, with a sea turtle, a shark's tooth, and a palm tree. If she could spare the money, she'd buy it for herself. A symbol of her new life, away from Alabama and Orin.

She gave her head a little shake and bent down to look at the candy. After the long hours in the car and the strangeness of setting up housekeeping in a women's shelter, they all needed a treat. And candy was cheap.

"You don't want that ordinary stuff, ma'am," said the tall, stoop-shouldered clerk. "Y'all be wanting some pralines for your boys." As he spoke, he slid three caramel-colored candies into a bag. "And for you..." He plucked the necklace she'd been studying from the stand and held it out to her.

"Oh, no! We can't afford all that!" What was *this* guy's agenda?

He smiled with an expression of wisdom and sympathy older than his years. "Just consider it a little southern hospitality. Y'all look like you be needing a lift."

For some reason, she trusted him. Maybe this was all going to work out. "Thank you. You're very kind."

She'd just taken the bag and turned to locate the boys when she felt something poke into her side. A familiar, sickeningly strong cologne assaulted her, and her heart started to pound.

Orin.

Silent terror exploded inside her, making her head spin and her stomach heave with nausea. She looked around frantically. There were Liam and Cash, fingering the crocodile heads on sticks. But where was her oldest, Sean? He had to get the other boys to safety, now.

How, oh how had Orin found them so quickly? And what new punishment would he inflict on her and, worse, on the boys?

"Thought you were going to leave me, did you?"

"Everything okay, Miss?" the clerk asked from behind her.

"You tell him it's fine and come with me," Orin said into her ear, "Or I'll kill him, and then those worthless boys, and then you."

She nodded back to the clerk, forcing a sick smile across her face. "I'm fine." Her chest seemed to crumple inward, as if all the backbone she'd tried to build in herself, all her bones, turned to jelly.

Her dreams and plans to save her children turned to dust.

Orin pulled her along like they were normal people in a hurry, jamming a gun into her side. As he reached the pickup and opened the door to shove her inside, she saw Sean, squatting on the sidewalk, caught up in his favorite battered military novel, one of the few possessions he'd insisted on bringing along when they'd fled Alabama.

There were people out on the street, shopping and chatting. Should she scream? Or would that incite Orin to a shooting spree? He was shaking, his face red with fury. She'd never seen him this bad. Her head spun, her heart pounding with great, heart-attack-like thuds.

Think. No. She couldn't expect help from strangers—not without endangering them and the kids, too—but she had to get Sean's attention. "Oh, Orin, you don't have to be in such a hurry!" she cried in a loud, fake voice.

Sean looked up, and their eyes met, and then his gaze turned to Orin. Bleak understanding darkened his eyes. Always protective, he scrambled to his feet and started to come toward her and Orin, but she glared and gave a sideways jerk of her head, indicating that he should go to his brothers, help them first, as she'd drilled into him on the ride up from Alabama.

He looked back, biting his lip, and every tendon sung with

the need to go to him, to hold him and tell him not to worry, she'd take care of it. As a mother should.

But she couldn't take care of this. He was only twelve, but today, he had to be a man and protect his brothers from their father. Her stomach ached like knives were stabbing it and her vision dimmed. She'd failed as a mother.

Sean squared his thin shoulders and headed toward the other two boys, who were play fighting inside the store, now armed with toy swords. Tears filled her eyes to witness their last minute of carefree childhood.

Then she was shoved headfirst into the pickup truck and the door closed behind her.

Three hours later, sore in every public and private part of her body, she fell from the truck to the side of the road, limp as a rag doll, barely feeling the gravel dig into her elbow and cheek.

"You wanted to live here, you can die here." Orin's voice was dim, and then the truck door slammed. There was a roar and the truck drove away.

Her consciousness was fading, her vision blurring.

She tried to move. Couldn't.

Tractor-trailers roared past on the highway, but none of them stopped. Maybe no one could see her. It was getting dark.

Liam was scared of the dark. Who would he turn to when he had a nightmare? Who would teach Cash the right values, how to be more generous? How would Sean have a childhood now?

Her thoughts circled, becoming more distant. Something burned her eyes, and she realized, vaguely, that she was crying. Crying for all the mothering she wouldn't get to give to her sons.

A vehicle was coming, a truck. She clawed at the gravel and managed to heave herself closer to the pavement. Another claw to the gravel, another heave. She had to get help, had to get to her boys. She pushed herself up on one bloody elbow, tried to lift a hand to wave to the truck as its headlights beamed so bright that she reeled backwards. Pain made her stomach heave, and blackness dimmed the edges of her vision.

She pushed herself up higher. "Hey!" she tried to call out.

The truck thundered on past her and she collapsed down again.

Her head hurt like the worst headache she'd ever had, times ten.

She hadn't wanted it to end this way, but somehow, she'd always known it would.

~

Twenty years later

Chapter One

Sean O'Dwyer looked around the lived-in bayou cottage where he'd spent his teenage years, rubbed the back of his neck, and dug deep for patience. Nothing like your childhood home to make you feel like a rebellious teenager.

Especially when you'd never wanted to return to the town that had always seen your family as second best. Or third, or tenth. But Safe Haven was known as a place where you could lick your wounds in peace, and while that primarily applied to women, a handful of men had gotten their footing here, too.

Maybe he'd be one of them. He had nothing left to lose.

"Living by yourself out there in the salt marshes isn't going to make you feel any better." Ma Dixie, the woman who'd taken him in when he was an angry thirteen-year-old and raised him up to be a decent man, glanced over from clearing the lunch dishes, her broad face wrinkled with concern. "You could just as well plan the renovation staying right here with me."

Liam, who at twenty-eight was the youngest of Sean's motley crew of adopted and biological brothers, leaned back against Ma's kitchen counter and sipped sweet tea. "Your ex-wife was worried you'd do something rash."

Sean blinked. "You talked to Gabby? You *listened* to her?"

Liam spread his hands and shrugged. "She was concerned."

"Concerned enough to dump me for her fertility doctor," Sean muttered, and then was sorry he had. He didn't need their pitying looks. And truly, he and Gabby had grown so far apart after his two tours in Afghanistan that there hadn't been much of a marriage left. Throw in infertility, and the whole thing had blown up in his face.

He didn't even miss her, not really. He just missed the hope he'd felt, getting married. That an O'Dwyer could overcome his past, be a happy husband and father who treated his family well and was loved in return. His throat tightened and he shoved aside that stupid dream. "I'm caretaking the place, too. Eldora was afraid kids or vandals would break into the cottages."

Liam studied him steadily. "When I heard you were coming home, I thought you'd find a way to help the shelter. It's not doing so well."

"That's your department." Liam was a police officer and lived smack in the middle of Safe Haven.

"Your brother's got his hands full. Looking at a promotion to chief." Ma smiled at Liam with fond pride. She hadn't raised him or their brother Cash, when their family had fallen apart. Her small bayou house had only had room for Sean, but her heart had always been big enough to consider both of Sean's natural brothers as kin. And although Liam and Cash had landed in different local families, both of them looked at Ma Dixie's cabin as a second home.

Sean lifted an eyebrow. "Congratulations. Never thought my little brother would end up the top guy."

His brother punched his arm, none too lightly. "Thanks for the vote of confidence. Where's Cash, Ma? I thought he was supposed to help us talk sense into Stupid, here."

"Sean's not stupid. And Cash called. Some high-flying deal, so he's stuck in Atlanta." Ma Dixie pulled the shades to block the afternoon sun, then put her hands on ample hips. "I agree with Liam. You ought to stay in town, figure out a way to help the shelter, not go off and lick your wounds alone. Eldora can find another caretaker."

Sean ignored the wounds part. "I'm no use to the shelter." *Just like the shelter had been no use to their mother.* "Do I look like the kind of guy a battered woman would trust?"

"You could clean yourself up." Ma pinched his bristly cheek. "Shave. Cut your hair."

"Lighten up on the steroids," Liam joked, then raised a hand when Sean bristled. "I know, you wouldn't. But you're huge! You must've been working out 24/7."

Sean didn't bother to disabuse his brother of that notion. The truth was, he'd been doing hard physical labor back in Knoxville, working construction alongside his team. Partly to pay for the divorce, and partly to keep his mind off of things.

But the noise and chatter had gotten to him. It was getting to him now. He stood. "If the intervention's over," he said, "I've got a job to do."

"You'll come for Friday night suppers, now that you're back in the area?"

"Sure, Ma." He put an arm around the woman and squeezed her shoulders. He owed her his life and would lay it on the line for her or any one of his brothers. Outsiders, not so much. "Don't worry about me. I'm going to be fine. I just need a little peace and quiet."

~

Sea Pine Cottages: Closed for Summer Renovations.

Anna George stopped the car in front of a pair of padlocked gates, stared at the sign, and then let her forehead rest briefly on the steering wheel. What was she going to do now?

This whole, mad cross-country journey had been a terrible mistake.

"Mommy? Are we there yet?" Hailey's voice piped up from the back seat.

Uh-oh. When one twin woke up, so did the other, and patience wasn't a virtue most five-year-olds possessed. Anna needed a plan, fast.

She knew no one in South Carolina—which was the point—but as she and the twins had fled the cold mountains of Montana, she'd told them all about the low country's cute, friendly little towns, salt marshes, and warm, welcoming beaches. Right now, though, the closed gates in front of them blocked the first step of her plan.

"Mommy?" Hope was awake now, too, and her voice sounded anxious. "Where are we?"

"Let me think a minute." Anna reached a hand to the back seat and gave each girl a reassuring leg-pat. After what they'd seen and heard, they needed to know that they were safe, and that she was safe, and that she had a plan.

There were nice hotels, farther down the coast, but prices were high. And the kind of small motels she could afford didn't offer the privacy she needed.

Her stomach twisted and turned, but she didn't dare panic. She wiped wet palms down the sides of her shorts and studied the sign again. If the park was closed for renovations, they had to be renovating *something*. Ideally, the cabins she remembered from her sole, idyllic childhood vacation. And, God willing, the renovations wouldn't have started yet and would happen at a slow Southern pace. Or maybe never; sometimes places put up an optimistic "Reopening Soon!" sign when it was doubtful they'd ever do business again.

The twins were murmuring in their abbreviated secret language, and they apparently reached a conclusion. "We want *out* of the car!"

"Okay. One minute." She put the car in reverse, backed up, and pulled off to the side of the gates where shiny azalea bushes grew thick and high. She eased deep into a hollow section, well-sheltered from the road and entrance. Grabbed a couple of tools from the glove box.

You can do this, Anna. You don't have a choice.

"Come on, girls," she said, forcing cheer into her voice. "Let's go exploring!"

Fifteen minutes later, they'd ascertained that there were no construction machines, no signs of workers. The place was deserted, which suited Anna just fine. From the road, they scouted the row of tumbledown cabins and selected the sturdiest-looking one.

"Come on, it's going to be an adventure!" She pushed sweaty hair out of her eyes and urged the girls up the overgrown path toward the cabin. This had to work.

"I don't like bugs!" Hope, always more fearful and fretful, waved away a cloud of tiny sand flies and leaned into Anna's leg, making it hard to walk.

"I'm first!" Hailey, as usual, ran ahead, reaching the door of the tumbledown cabin and turning the handle. "It's locked, Mom," she said, tossing back her blonde ringlets. "Where's the key?"

"That's the adventure part." Tugging Hope along, Anna reached the door and knelt to study the lock, putting an arm around both girls. She'd hoped for an old-fashioned bolt she could just slide a screwdriver under, but this lock was modern and tight.

That would be better in the long run, safer.

Who'd have thought that law-abiding, rule-following Anna Smith would calmly break and enter? She shoved down the eddy of fear, of wondering what would happen if they got caught. It wasn't a lifestyle she wanted to participate in long-term, and she certainly didn't want to teach it to the girls.

But for now, she'd do what she had to for their safety.

Around them, birds had resumed their chirping and cawing. The salt air blew warm, bringing the fragrance of the sea, just beyond the dunes if her childhood memories served. In fact, if she closed her eyes, she imagined she could hear it: the rhythmic pounding of waves against the sand.

"Mommy? What're we going to do?" Hope's voice trembled.

"I'm hungry," Hailey complained.

But at least they were speaking. And Anna meant to make sure that continued, that their voices weren't silenced as they'd been in the past.

She stood, stepped back. "Let's take a walk around the cabin."

"Yeah!" Hailey started to rush off.

"Wait. What's the rule?"

Her impulsive daughter stopped. "Stay together," she said reluctantly.

"That's right, good job," Anna said to Hailey, and then looked down at Hope's anxious face. Though her twins were identical physically, their personalities were nearly opposite. "Want a ride on my back, kiddo?"

"Okay."

Anna knelt. "Jump up." When Hope did, Anna staggered to her feet. Blackness started to close her vision, but she grabbed the trunk of a live oak tree and steadied herself, took a couple of deep breaths. No sleep and a boatload of worries were wearing her down, but she'd gotten this far. She could do this.

She looked up at the cloud-mottled sky. "Okay, let's take a look."

They made their way around the small cabin. Up close, she could see that time and neglect had taken their toll. Part of the screen that sheltered the porch was ripped, and white siding curved away from the cabin, warped by weather. She let Hailey slip through the torn screen to test the cabin's back door, but it was locked, too.

They continued on around. Mushrooms, bold red and yellow, sprouted in the sandy soil near the small picnic table. No footprints, no trash, no abandoned beach toys.

The loneliness chilled her, but it was what she and the girls needed, at least for now. And the cabin's basic structure seemed sound. "Peek inside," she urged Hope, moving closer to a promising window.

Hope hesitated, then leaned from her perch on Anna's back to peer into the window. "It's got a kitchen table! And a sofa and chairs."

Perfect. As long as the furniture hadn't become a nest for rodents or bugs, but she'd keep that fear to herself. Her girls' safety was more important than perfect hygiene.

On the third side of the cabin, Anna found what she was searching for: a low window that looked loose in its frame. "Slide down, sweetie. I want you and Hailey to walk out to the road and back. Count the steps."

"But what if it's more than a hundred?" Hope asked. That was as high as the twins could count.

"Then we'll start over." Hailey grabbed her twin's hand and tugged. "Come on!"

As the girls headed toward the road, squabbling, Anna pulled a screwdriver out of her back pocket and eased it between the sill and the window edge. Working quickly, she jiggled the window open enough to get leverage and then wedged the screwdriver in. The wood was swollen and tight, but she manhandled it upward with brute strength she hadn't known she had.

If she didn't find shelter for the night, and longer, she feared that unfixable damage that might come to her children. Sleeping in the car, tangling with the drifters who hung around roadside rest areas and truck stops. No.

And the ultimate fear: that Beau would find them.

The window broke free in a rush and sped upward, splintering the sill. A long needle of painted wood dug into her hand. She pulled it out, wincing, and leaned into the room.

Musty, but that could be fixed with open windows, as long as the slight breeze kept up. She heard skittering feet, saw a shadow race across the floor. Small and compact: probably a mouse. Mice she could handle. She just prayed there were no snakes.

Most important, she didn't see any signs of human habitation: no stacks of clothes, no dishes on the little kitchen counter. She didn't want to disturb another squatter. Didn't trust such a person, even though she was about to become one herself.

She couldn't believe that keeping her children safe had come to this.

For the thousandth time on their three-day pilgrimage, she questioned whether she'd made the right decisions. Leaving Beau, yes. And her job, telemarketing from home, hadn't been a reason to stay in Montana. But heading to the South Carolina coast, based on a town's name and some hazy childhood memories? That had been impulsive.

On the other hand, where else could she have gone? Her father didn't have had a lick of spare energy for her problems, and the few others in her extended family weren't close enough to turn to.

"Mom! It was seventy-eight steps!"

"No, eighty!"

The twins rushed to her, red-faced and bedraggled, and she knelt and hugged them fiercely, one in each arm, inhaling their sweaty-kid scent. They needed baths, or at least a swim, soon. She was just thankful that they were safe and with her.

"Whatcha doing with that window?" Hailey asked.

"Are we allowed to open it?" Hope looked worried.

"It'll be fine," she said to Hope. "You'll see what I'm doing in a minute. But for now, I want you to go stand on the front porch, and close your eyes, and count to...."

"Fifty!"

"A hundred!"

"Seventy-five," Anna said. "Go on. Scoot." It was a good thing they'd arrived in South Carolina, because she was running out of creative games to keep the girls entertained.

Hoisting herself up, she flung a leg through the waist-high window and eased through the casement, scraping her thigh on the rough wood. Blood beaded bright against her fading, yellow-green bruises.

She was in. She dusted her hands together, did a quick inspection to assure herself that the place was solid and safe, and threw the front door open just as the girls shouted "seventy-five" together. "Come see our new vacation home!"

They walked in, wide-eyed but accepting, and the three of them explored the small cabin. Faded, vinyl-covered camp mattresses remained on rusty cots, a single in one bedroom and a double in another. The living room was fully, if shabbily, furnished, and the pine paneling on the walls gave the place a cozy, old-fashioned feel.

"Where's the stove?" Hailey asked.

"And the fridge?" Hope added.

Anna came into the kitchen area and looked around, putting her hands on her hips. "They were taken out because people don't live here anymore. But we'll be fine. We have our cooler, and we can cook things on our camp stove."

"Or just eat cereal," Hope added helpfully.

Anna blew out a breath. "No. We're going to start having real meals again, just as soon as we can go to the grocery store." If memory served, there was a small one in the coastal village of Safe Haven, just a few miles down the road. For more supplies, they'd take the highway to Myrtle Beach.

"Hey, the lights don't work!" Hailey stood flicking the light switch in the kitchen. Hope ran to check the one in the living room, and then the girls ran from switch to switch, testing each one and getting the same result.

Anna tried the faucet: no water. Of course. She should have expected that once she'd realized that the rustic little resort wasn't open for business. Electricity they could do without, but they needed water.

She let the twins run as she looked around, planning. A worried glance out the window showed a low-hanging sun, so she had to get moving. They'd bring in what they needed, light the lantern, get out dinner. Probably peanut-butter sandwiches, but she'd fix the girls some fruit at least. She'd locate a flashlight and go hunting for the main water valve, set the girls to work wiping down mattresses. They'd find a broom and sweep up the dead bugs and other questionable litter on the floor. For tonight, they'd be okay.

Tomorrow, she'd deal with the fact that she was in a strange state where she knew no one, with two little girls to support on very limited funds. She'd figure out their next step.

She shot up a prayer of thanks for the fact that they'd found refuge. They were beginning a new life without Beau, and for now at least, they were safe. That was all that mattered.

∼

After loading up his truck with supplies from the hardware store—and a twelve-pack of beer to wash away the taste of his family's annoying interference—Sean O'Dwyer pulled up to the closed gates of the Sea Pine Cottages, rolled down his window, and just sat for a minute, enjoying the moonlight.

The vibrating hum of cicadas rose and fell, and in the distance, waves pounded. The southern breeze that cooled his face felt like home, as did the looming cedar and live-oak trees draped spookily with Spanish moss. Marshy salt-smells reminded him of long days spent canoeing through the area's blackwater rivers.

The low country would heal him. It always did.

And living here, alone, would be enough for him.

He got out of his car, keyed open the padlock, and unwound the chain. He was pushing the squeaky, rusty gate open when the hair on the back of his neck rose.

Something was out of place.

His heart rate accelerated as he stepped back to his truck to retrieve his pistol, then did a deliberately slow 360. His intuition for danger had been honed on the streets of Kabul and he knew better than to ignore it, even in these much-more-peaceful surroundings.

There. A flash.

He walked quietly toward it and realized there was a car parked behind the bushes that framed the gate. Decently hidden, but not to someone with his experience. A small Hyundai sedan that had seen better days. Hand on his weapon, he approached it.

It was empty. But most cars held some evidence of their owners—a potato chip bag, kid toys, a spare jacket or sweater. This one was completely clean. Almost as if its owner didn't want it to reveal anything.

It was too dinged up to be a rental. So the car owner really came from Montana.

He felt the hood. Cold.

He got back in his truck and let it roll silently down toward the cabin he'd been working on and living in, closest to the beach, already mostly renovated. As he rode, he scanned the darkness.

There. A light. Bobbing up and down inside cabin #3, just two doors down from the tumbledown beachfront one he'd selected for himself. Somebody must think they could get a vacation for free. Either that, or they were up to something illegal. Between Kabul and Knoxville, he'd learned to trust no one.

He coasted past, parked the truck, and headed back toward the cabin with the light. He'd figured some locals would disregard the "Keep Out" signs, but he'd been expecting partying teenagers. A single flashlight suggested someone with more nefarious aims.

He approached the cabin slowly, watching, listening.

The light was off now, either that or it had moved to another room.

He shuffled through nettles and hackberry, glad for his work boots, looking in the windows. There was stuff that shouldn't be there, barely visible in the moonlight. A carton of food in the kitchen, a cooler, a couple of suitcases. Someone was intending to settle in.

But that wasn't happening, not on his watch. He came around to the back porch of the cabin and lifted aside a broken section of the screen. Used his knife to slit it the rest of the way open. Stepped cautiously through.

The slight, silent figure that rose in front of him gave him two seconds of warning, and he ducked, but not soon enough.

Fire stung his eyes and he staggered backward, his skin burning. He grabbed his assailant's slender wrist and pulled her down with him.

ABOUT THE AUTHOR

Lee Tobin McClain is the New York Times bestselling author of more than thirty novels. A professor-turned-writer, she finds inspiration in her beautiful and brilliant daughter, her goofy goldendoodle, and her aptly named cat, Trouble. For more about Lee and her books, visit her website at www.leetobinmcclain.com.

Sign up for Lee's newsletter and receive a free novella!
www.leetobinmcclain.com

Copyright © 2016 by Lee Tobin McClain.

All rights reserved. No part of this publication may be reproduced, distributed or transmitted in any form or by any means, including photocopying, recording, or other electronic or mechanical methods, without the prior written permission of the publisher, except in the case of brief quotations embodied in critical reviews and certain other noncommercial uses permitted by copyright law. For permission requests, write to the publisher, addressed "Attention: Permissions Coordinator," at the address below.

tobin@setonhill.edu
    www.leetobinmcclain.com

Publisher's Note: This is a work of fiction. Names, characters, places, and incidents are a product of the author's imagination. Locales and public names are sometimes used for atmospheric purposes. Any resemblance to actual people, living or dead, or to businesses, companies, events, institutions, or locales is completely coincidental.

Sacred Bond Guardians Vol. 1-3 plus prequel Novella /
    Lee Tobin McClain. -- 1st ed.

Made in United States
Cleveland, OH
16 April 2025